D1030982

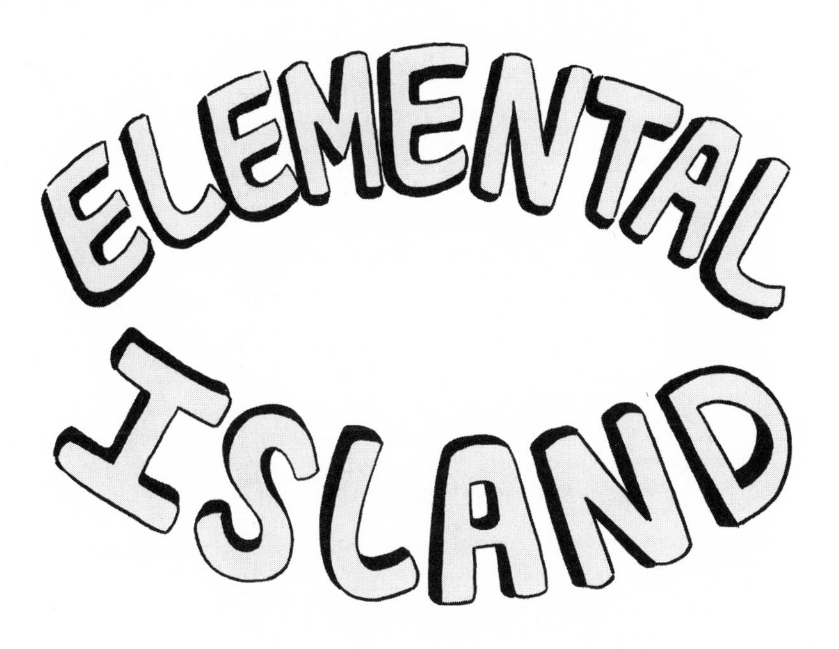

KATHY HOOPMANN

J.S. KISS

Jessica Kingsley *Publishers*
London and Philadelphia

First published in 2016
by Jessica Kingsley Publishers
73 Collier Street
London N1 9BE, UK
and
400 Market Street, Suite 400
Philadelphia, PA 19106, USA

www.jkp.com

Library of Congress Cataloging in Publication Data
A CIP catalog record for this book is available from the Library of Congress

British Library Cataloguing in Publication Data
A CIP catalogue record for this book is available from the British Library

ISBN 978 1 84905 658 8
eISBN 978 1 78450 228 7

Printed and bound in the United States

To

Shani, who would want to leave the island too,
and
Abigail, who approves of bacon-flavoured molecular gel

With a huge thanks to our pre-readers for their insight and advice. This book is much the richer for their input. Dylan Hamilton, child editor extraordinaire, and his amazing mum, Rachel Hamilton, Ryan Kilpadi, Kay Bridges, Karl Hoopmann, Rebecca Houkamau, Jacqueline Truesdale and Marie and David Oldfield.

Contents

1

Blue and Wet Behind the Ears

"Jakob! Pass the ball!" I yelled.

He stood still, gazing at the sky.

"Sal, kick it!" She gave a half-hearted try. "No! Your goal is at the other end!"

A Labrador bounded out of nowhere and wanted to join in. Frankly, I wouldn't have minded, since at least *it* seemed to be enjoying itself. Michio was terrified of dogs though.

"Michio, watch out!" I cried. He clambered up the nearest tree and clung to a branch, whimpering.

The dog nipped at the ball, covering more of the field than we had during the whole game. Wish it were on my team! Then I saw where it was heading.

"Jakob, help!"

Too late.

The dog ran onto the road in front of a truck that swerved to avoid it. The back door swung open spilling colourful rolls of 3D filaments all over the kerb and into the front yards of the houses. So many things to chase!

"Hold on!" I yelled to a woman up a ladder, painting her house. The Labrador crashed headfirst into the rungs and toppled a can of blue paint. A cat yowled and I caught a flash of a blue tail.

"Catch him!" a man spluttered as he ran towards the mess, swinging a leash.

Jakob and I sprinted after the dog who thought this was the best game yet. Slipping and sliding in the blue paint we finally managed to hold it long enough for the man to fasten the clip on the collar.

"Sorry," I said.

"Sorry?" he growled. "Is this your fault?"

I looked around. No way was I taking the blame for this. Okay, I did organise the game but no one, not even the statistics teacher, could have predicted this mayhem.

Once again, my attempt at making friends had failed. It was not fair. The day was scheduled in everyone's calpads weeks ahead – with daily reminders. To get them to come, I told them that I was investigating a theory for my major thesis. I was turning twelve in a less than a week and hadn't a clue what to do. My name was the only one down in the class calpad as *Undecided*. So I pretended I was investigating the effects of gravity on the path of an object that's thrown or launched. I even memorised $d = vt$ to sound convincing.

Really, all I wanted was a game of football. It sounded fun: kicking a ball, cheering on your team. I knew from history investigation classes that it took more than four people to play it, but I was thrilled that three others had agreed to join me. But nothing I had read warned me how dangerous football could be.

The dog owner marched away mumbling under his breath as the Monitors arrived. A man and a woman in baggy black uniforms with reflector strips across their chest borrowed the painter's ladder and extended it up the tree to rescue Michio. Michio was still crying. He had a very low pain threshold and those bark burns must have been agony for him.

A couple of cars drove past us, small hisses emitting from the cold fusion engines as the drivers slowed down to see what was going on. Once back on the ground, Michio pointed our way. I gulped.

Sal came up behind me. "If I get into trouble for this, I'm totally blaming you." Then, before slipping into the crowd that was gathering, she whispered, "Your game is as stupid as your name."

Astatine was one of the rarest elements from the periodic table. My mother thought it was a sweet and unique name for her daughter, ignoring the fact that

Astatine is so rare that it has no use outside of scientific research. My "friends" never failed to remind me of that. I called myself Astie, which sounded much more like a human name than a decomposing radioactive element, but only Grandmother and occasionally Jakob went along with it.

The clean-up crew arrived in their truck and began to spray the spilled paint until it congealed and was easy to scoop up.

"You are a sorry pair," one of the cleaners chuckled. "Unfortunately, this spray won't work so well on your skin. But we can try."

Jakob and I stood with our hands covering our faces as he turned the hose on us. Our hydrophobic clothes had drip dried clean by the time one of the Monitors started questioning us.

"So, let me get this straight," he said after I explained what had happened. "You played a game that involved kicking a ball at your friends. Couldn't that harm them?"

"Not if they kicked it back," I retorted, turning to Jakob. "Why did you just stand there?"

"I was thinking about terraforming planets, like they did in Space Seekers."

The Monitor looked up at the clouds. "I guess you could seed an atmosphere with algae," he suggested, "unless there was sulphuric acid present."

I groaned. I was the only child I knew who did not think a show about a spaceship lost on the other side of the galaxy was the most fascinating digicast in the world. I tried to keep focused on the important stuff.

"My birthday is next week." I raised my voice to get his attention. "I was investigating a theory for my thesis."

The Monitor nodded. "A very worthy cause, with unfortunate results," he said, then wrote up something into his calpad and slapped it back around his wrist. The band of clear plastic moulded to his skin and I could see his hairs beneath it. Both my and Jakob's calpads chimed and I knew his report had been submitted.

"We'll be more careful next time," I called to him as he walked away.

"I am not convinced there will be a next time," Jakob said, reading the report. Sure enough, at the end of the note it read, *"Although events were unpredictable, future attempts at 'football games' are not advised."*

Jakob and I walked home together. Pale grey hexagonal solar cells lined the pavement of this street, the result of someone's thesis years ago before cold fusion took over. Our shoes clacked on the hard plastic surface and I was glad when the cells ended, replaced by hardy wear-resistant grass. We walked past Rainbow Square. Spiralling metal swirls hung from poles, and crystals were embedded into the paving stones. In full sunlight, the square reflected rainbows from lots of different surfaces. A giant machine in the middle spewed bubbles of all sizes and colours in every direction from hoops, high and low. Usually, a small cluster of people would sit mesmerised. This close to the evening meal, the square was deserted. I swung my fist at a large purplish bubble that flew my way. Jakob looked at me puzzled, and then he figured it out. "You are still upset about the game. I'm sorry I messed it up for you."

"It's not just the game, Jakob. My life is messed up."

"That is not correct. You have all your basic needs met, and more. You have food and shelter, you are safe, your parents love you and you have time to explore your interests."

Trust Jakob to be practical.

"Yeah, right. Except my interests are nothing like everyone else's."

"You are who you are, Astie. I like that you are different."

I snorted. "You are the only one who does."

"Then you have one friend. Without me, your life would be 100 per cent worse."

Jakob's facts drove me crazy most of the time, but this time I laughed. We had grown up together. His father and mine were brothers, which meant that we were listed in the relations registry as *Forbiddens* who could never marry, but neither of us would want to do that anyway.

I heard a soft chime and glanced at my wrist. A display lit up with a warning. Evening meal in twenty minutes.

"We'd better hurry," Jakob said.

"Last one home is a rotten egg!" I called out as I ran ahead.

"That is not logical!" Jakob said, but gave chase anyway. We raced past identical houses that you could tell apart by special interests displayed in the yards; purple grass, a cluster of windmills, luminescent garden furniture, half-finished projects that curled and spiked and could be anything from an omelette maker to an attempted invisibility machine. You name it; someone in this town has tried to make it.

Dogs barked at us and banged headfirst into transparent fences as they tried to snap at our heels. Dumb mutts. You would think they'd learn. I managed to stay ahead of Jakob until we reached our corner. My house was easy to spot as it had Father's cat carvings decorating the lawn. Father's third obsession was felines. It had been his twelve-year-old thesis and he is still on it thirty years later. I ran up to my front door, which slid open for me. Jakob jogged on to his house at the end of the street.

By the time I got to the kitchen, Mother had started programming the food printer. Father and my brother Jon sat at the table waiting.

"So Zero Six," Jon said, "Michio sent me a cally telling me you were *feeling blue* today."

I cringed. Jon has called me Zero Six ever since he found out that to keep our population stable, families needed 2.06 children. He decided that he was worth two and my brain was only 0.06 per cent there.

"Don't insult your sister," Mother said automatically.

"Blue?" Father echoed Jon. "Are you feeling sad, Astatine?"

"No," Jon chuckled, "I don't mean the idiom, Father. She was literally blue *and* wet behind the ears." He laughed at his own joke.

I rued the time I developed an interest in archaic speech patterns and taught the whole family some silly sayings. Jon teases me about them all the time.

"Didn't you read the cally from the Monitors, Stephen?" Mother asked. Father was always too busy with his cats to worry about day-to-day stuff. He touched his wrist and read the note. Then he said, "That was an unexpected outcome, Astatine. I am glad that no one got hurt."

"Astatine is weird. Unexpected outcomes are to be expected around her."

"They are not!" I retorted.

"Stop calling your sister weird." Mother brought the steak, potatoes and broccoli to the table. Jon hated the texture of most food, and as usual, he'd opted for molecular gel reshaped to resemble the meal it had originally been. Brown, white and green blobs quivered on his plate.

"Astatine, would you like me to request that you be allowed to continue your investigations into the ballistic trajectory of a projectile?"

For a moment, I wondered what Mother was talking about, then she added, "After all, it is the first thesis possibility you have considered in a long time and you have to decide on one very soon."

"Oh that," I said. "No. Don't bother. It doesn't matter." Mother still refused to acknowledge that I was considering fashion for my thesis.

Jon burst out laughing.

"What?"

"If a ball didn't *matter* it would have no mass and it would go at the speed of light!" he spluttered.

Father chuckled and even Mother gave a quick grin.

I turned away in disgust. I swear, I think I was dropped on this island from another planet!

2

In Danger of Becoming Mildly Interesting

Although it was still early, the air was already hot as I stepped outside. Jakob was coming up to the gate to meet me, as he did every morning, five days a week. He wore his usual navy T-shirt and baggy black pants and his dark brown hair was shorn as always. But today something was different, and that didn't happen very often on the island.

Jakob was floating in the air!

"What…?" I managed to squeak.

He was surrounded by a small group of people calling out techie questions that included words like reverse electromagnetism, non-ferromagnetic conductors, electromechanical fluid separation and energy harnessing.

Curious about the noise, Jon came out and stood beside me. His jaw dropped. "Now that's what I call floating a good idea!" he called out, and the one or two people who understood him, smiled.

Jakob spotted us and waved. "It's the boots."

I gave him the thumbs up. Jakob's father, my Uncle Luke, had been working on creating hover boots ever since he saw them on a Space Seekers episode. Now he watched as his son spiralled and flipped in mid-air as if on an invisible trampoline. Luke's crazy white hair, messy on a good day, was now sticking out at all angles. Every person in town would want those boots. Gosh, even I was planning to sign up for hover classes. There must have been eight excited onlookers, whose calpad alarms were chiming reminding them of their schedules, but for once, no one cared. I guessed Jakob would not be walking me to the Learning Hub today. I did have a very important question about the boots, but I could ask him later.

I left the crowd and their unintelligible queries and headed for the Hub. Since Jakob was not with me, I decided to change my route and I wandered down the streets closer to the sea. There was a salt tang to the air and gulls swooped on the gentle breeze. Wispy clouds fractured like the lace I sometimes 3D printed for my designs. The Beach Park featured a full-sized disc-shaped vehicle, like the one that appeared in Space Seekers. I might loathe the show but when we were younger, Jakob and I slid down the steep sides of the disc all the time. I leaned against its sun-warmed metal and watched a sloth with greenish fur in a tree above me. It hung by two legs as it reached for the choicest broad leaf, then wrapped its long arms around a limb and started to chomp. Sloths weren't native to Elemental Island, but then nothing was. A few hundred years ago, it bubbled up as molten lava, the result of an underground eruption. Not that you'd know it now unless you went up to the meadows and saw the exposed black rock on the cliff faces on the way. The original settlers voted on which animals to introduce to the ecosystem, and for some reason the sloth was included. Perhaps they liked the way it could concentrate for hours on its special interests – sleeping and eating.

My great-great-grandparents on both sides had been original settlers. Elemental Harvesters, as they called themselves. They worked on breaking down materials to their elements to restructure them in 2D form. That's why they named the place Elemental Island and my dad's side of the family even took the surname, Harvester. When they first came, there was nothing here but grass and a few trees that had been seeded by wild birds. What an adventure that must have been! A bunch of scientists on a new island, who got to decide what species would live here.

A bird tweeted furiously by the creek and I wondered what it was scolding. I hoped it was none of our cats, although it could be a stray. I took the sand track through the ferns and saw a girl with a ponytail crouching by the water filling a metal flask. I thought she must be testing the water quality, but then she raised it to her lips and drank.

Ew. Think of the germs!

She must have heard me because she spun around. She was a he. A boy with long hair!

We eyeballed each other for an instant before he took off for the bushes and disappeared from sight.

"Hey!" I called. "Wait!" I was about to follow him when my calpad chimed. Drat! My learning session was starting in eighteen minutes. I couldn't afford another demerit mark. Let's just say that Teacher and I don't always see things the same way. The mystery boy would have to wait. I started jogging and took a short cut through the park of yesterday's disaster. Neil, the mower man, made grass an art. Not a single weed, or burr or ant marred his field and families could picnic on a surface soft as fur. As I drew closer, I saw a Monitor van parked in the middle of the field. This was the third unexpected event of the day. Nothing out of the ordinary happens for months, and now three things in one morning! The island was in danger of becoming mildly interesting.

As I drew closer, I saw tyre marks in the pristine lawn. Neil was not going to be happy. That grass was his life. Sure enough, he was standing next to his mower, flapping his chubby hands. His face was bright red and his eyes bulged as he rocked backwards and forwards on the spot. The Monitors knew better than to touch him in this state, but they were watching him.

Neil was a Level One. Level Ones had obsessions that were simple, but vital to the community. They were very happy doing things other people didn't want to do much, like sweep streets and pick up leaves, often one at a time. Neil mowed the community parks five days a week. I knew him quite well as his father had helped mine with the original cat runs. When we were younger, Jakob and I called him Mr Round-and-Round, not only because he was, well let's face it, quite rotund, but also because he used to sing those words as he sat on his ride-on, mowing the grass.

Poor guy! Level Ones were easy to upset, and could take a long time to recover if they were not calmed. I ran up to him.

"Why did you park on Neil's grass?" I called to the Monitors. "You must have known that would set him off!"

A woman with long blonde hair in a braid turned and said, "He pressed his panic button. When we got here, we found bits of a compass scattered next to his mower." She held up a sealed elemental bag and I could see a base plate and the dial of the compass. "I tried to give it back to him, but he doesn't want it. Do you know him?"

"Yeah…" I began, but the other Monitor, a much older man with a unibrow, cut me off. "This is not your concern. Please resume your routine."

I was tempted to do just that since I was running so late. Monitors were highly trained, and dedicated to the job. They were also known for being intolerant of help from passers-by. Then Neil grabbed my arm in a fierce grip. I tried not to wince.

"Big bump," he spluttered, his eyes blinking fast, looking anywhere but me.

"You broke your compass?" I asked. "Don't worry, Neil. We can print you a new one."

He shook me by my arm. "Big bump," he repeated. His eyes fluttered and then focused on the mower.

"Maybe something is wrong with his ride-on?" I suggested.

The man started it up. "Seems fine to me," he said.

Neil's eyes swivelled at the barely audible hiss of the engine. "Mower," he said, a little calmer now. He let go and put the palm of his hand on the front of the hood.

I was glad to feel the blood return to my arm. "Why did you press your alarm?"

He paid no attention to me. As he rubbed the shiny, red surface of the machine, I noticed a small dent. So, that was what had upset him!

"The mower is fine. You can go mow," I said to Neil. "If that's okay with you?" I asked the Monitors.

"Sure," the woman nodded. "If it calms him down."

I could see the tension ease out of Neil's body. "Go mow," he said.

He climbed on his machine. "Go mow," he mouthed. "Go mow," as he drove off to start his cycle.

The woman watched him ride away. "Do you know if he has frequent meltdowns?"

"No. He's usually content and he loves to mow."

"At least he seems fine now. We'll stay a little longer and make sure he does not relapse."

"Your presence is no longer needed," the man said, stating the obvious.

"You're welcome," I muttered under my breath, and with a last glance at Neil, I headed for the Learning Hub. At the edge of the field, I noticed something flitting under the same tree that Michio had clung to yesterday. Curious, I went closer. There was a faded strip of material caught on a lower branch. I pulled it down. It was about as long as my height. What made me gasp though was the intricate pattern stitched in threads that had mostly held their colour. Vivid blues, greens and browns swirled over the surface. Then I realised it was a map. A map stitched by hand onto a scarf, with no names, just formations. How wonderful! Fashion ideas bombarded my mind. I could stitch practical designs onto clothing and surely, people would want to wear them. Where could this scarf come from? I had never seen anything like it. Why was it in a tree? I glanced across at Neil who was now riding away, happy. Did this have something to do with his meltdown? Could it have been caught in a sudden gust of wind and startled him? Even if it had, it did not explain its origins.

It crossed my mind to go back to the Monitors and show them what I'd found, but I knew they'd take the scarf off me and I did not want to part with it yet. Besides, that man made it clear my help was not wanted. I'd keep to the rules. Finders were not keepers. I *would* hand it in. Eventually. With a tinge of guilt, I stuffed the scarf into my pack and then jumped with fright when something above me began to hiss.

It took all my effort not to cry out. Had someone caught me already?

3

But Flight Is Forbidden

I took a deep breath, and glanced up. A fluffy grey cat with a distinct blue tail snarled down at me from a nearby sapling. I giggled with relief.

"Hey Cat. Sorry about yesterday. If you are here this afternoon I'll try to clean that tail."

I checked my calpad for the time. Nine minutes left! I took a deep breath and ran towards the Learning Hub. I wasn't the only one arriving at the last minute. Sheryl joined me and I stifled a sigh. Her special interest was weather.

"So did you hear the thunder yesterday evening?" she said. "I've never heard anything like it. It had this build-up roar and then it faded away," she prattled as we speed-walked.

"Gosh, thunder in the sky. How unexpected," I said, trying to keep a step in front of her.

"Exactly!" she pushed her long blonde hair from her face. "Everyone knows thunder is always paired with lightning. Except, there was no storm last night."

A voice behind us said, "I heard it too! It boomed over my house!" Andre joined us as we entered the building. He was into climate studies too. I grimaced in greeting but he snubbed me. He's hated me ever since I glued lace to his sling psychrometer and used it as a fan.

"It had to be intra-cloud lightning for sure. Or cloud to cloud," Andre suggested, "but the humidity is all wrong for cloud to ground."

"I didn't see any clouds though," Sheryl said.

I jogged ahead. They would not even realise I'd gone. The door of the group room slid open. It was noisier than normal in there. Everyone was clustered around Jakob, buzzing about the hover boots. He was already sitting in his place, legs extended, so people could take a good look at the mechanism on the soles. I slid into my pod next to his, the same one that had been mine since I started at the Hub when I was six.

"Father said it would be good advertising," he explained. "If there is a demand for them, the council will be more inclined to allocate the filaments to print them."

"They're amazing! What colours will they come in?" I said, getting to the essential question.

Jakob shook his head. "Your uncle just created the design of the century and all you can think of is fashion." He turned back to the learners on the other side of his pod.

Everybody in the Hub liked Jakob. In fact, most of the time people tolerated me because we were cousins. He had an amazing brain that could entertain people for hours. His greatest trick was to quote pi to 68,000 places. To be precise, it was 68,011 places, but I like to annoy him by rounding off things. He calcast himself doing it and it took him over twenty-four hours.

Now that the hover boots were causing a stir, he would be even more popular. Attempted inventions were commonplace and the town was littered with hope machines. People could spend their entire lives creating things that couldn't work. Either the technology had not been refined yet, or the materials were not available or the council simply deemed the inventions too dangerous. Uncle Luke's boots were functional though. He was bound to win an award.

I could see no awards in *my* future. I hated maths and physics and could only quote pi to 39 digits as it was compulsory learning. Without a doubt, I would never even use that knowledge, unless... I had a sudden thought. I could stitch it on something people wanted to wear! Taking off my calpad, I let it unfold and began doodling the hover boots. They may have been an amazing invention, but they were so ugly. I streamlined them a bit, which made an immediate improvement, then I wrote the numbers of pi in a spiral starting at the tip of the toe. It needed work but it was start. I had asked Teacher if I could do fashion design as my thesis, but he encouraged me to think about it more. Technically, no thesis was considered too trivial, but its result marked your place in society, and everyone knew that fashion would never make you popular. My new idea might change all that.

Teacher entered at 01:30 and everyone settled down for the two hours of compulsory learning that was to follow. For most children, general knowledge class was the time they dreaded the most, since the rest of the day they could explore their own interests. I couldn't understand why. It was my favourite part at the Hub. For starters, we met as a group. Fifteen people together! We all sat in separate pods but the sides were down so we could see each other and take part in the discussions. I hated it when the sides came up and we sat enclosed in our own little cocoons. It's not that I was claustrophobic, but it seemed such a waste. People that close, but I couldn't talk to them. If it wasn't for the fact that most of my fellow learners didn't like me, I could have spent all day, every day, learning in a group. Maybe that could be my thesis instead of fashion – I could make it sound impressive – the Correlation of Group Dynamics and Cognitive Development.

General Knowledge was my best subject and it was just my luck that no one else thought it was very important. The trick was that I didn't have to be obsessed with something to concentrate on it. Not a lot of people found that easy. But today, I was preoccupied.

"...Astatine?"

I glanced up at the voice. Teacher and the rest of the learners were staring at me.

"I asked if you know how many elements there are."

"One hundred and twenty," I said automatically.

"She'd know all about them," Andre said. "Especially the *unstable* ones."

The learners giggled but stopped when Teacher glared at them. He turned back to me.

"Correct, Astatine. But I would prefer that you put aside your calpad and give your attention to me."

"Are you drawing a HAt?" someone called out. Teacher's eyes swivelled around the room to see who had spoken, but all faces were innocent.

HAt is the molecular formula of hydrogen astatide, a compound of hydrogen and astatine. It was a very old joke and I didn't react. I wouldn't give them the satisfaction. How I wished Mother had given me a normal name!

Before I could erase anything, Sal reached over from her pod and snatched my calpad from my hands. "She's decorating the hover boots!" She held up the doodles for all to see.

"I wouldn't wear anything Astatine designed," Andre said. "It would only have a half-life of 8.3 hours!"

All the learners erupted in laughter.

"That's pi, isn't it," Jakob's voice cut through the noise. "I like the Fibonacci spiral."

Teacher raised his voice for once. "Silence! You know it is forbidden to mock another's special interests, and personal attributes."

The snickering died down.

"I was stating a fact," Sal pointed out.

"Facts are not accompanied by derisive laughter. Mind your manners!"

Manners were drilled into us from birth. They made my life bearable. Because of them, I wasn't teased or tormented much. Just ignored. There were no rules against ignoring other people. I got out of my pod and grabbed my calpad back from

Sal, staring so hard into her eyes that she flinched. I resisted the impulse to punch her. Getting physical would get me into much more trouble than name-calling. I slumped back into my pod and slammed the calpad on the fold-down writing table. "I wish I could leave Elemental Island and never come back!" I said under my breath. Unfortunately, many in my class had hypersensitive hearing and a few children snickered.

"That is an unreasonable expectation, Astatine," Teacher said. "Travel beyond the island is impossible."

"Not impossible," Sheryl said. "We *are* very far from the continents, but we could always build a boat. However, it is forbidden."

"Correction noted, Sheryl."

"We could always build a flight machine," Jakob added and there was more laughter.

Even Teacher cracked a smile at that. "Why is flight impossible for us?" he asked, turning to Jakob for the answer.

"The hypothesis is that our internal organs will explode at great heights."

"I heard that our eyeballs would pop out of their sockets," Sal added.

"I thought there was not enough air up there," someone else called out.

"Perhaps these points are all correct," Teacher agreed, "but they don't matter, Sheryl is right, of course. It is forbidden to leave the island. Tell me again why that is, children."

"Rule 1.1 For the safety of all inhabitants, it is forbidden to leave Elemental Island," the whole group chanted in unison.

4

If I Were a Zogart, No One in My Village Would Starve

Teacher gestured to the wall calpad. "As you can see, today is Konstantin's experimental session. Some of you may know him. He is in the nine-year-old learning group. He is investigating discomfort as an incentive."

"Like in Episode 162 of Space Seekers," Sheryl called out. "The Ferroblasters put food for the Zogarts next to the fire pit to see if they would risk walking on hot coals to save their village."

"Exactly," Teacher agreed. "Except none of you have to walk on hot coals."

The class burst into laughter. I never did understand their humour.

"I see that every one of you has gained parental approval to participate."

"Thanks, Mother." I stifled a groan. I had even wiped the reminder note for the permission from my own calpad, but trust Mother to check the Learning Hub notices.

"Now, remember what we practised. Do not exceed your own pain threshold."

"Bet you don't last a minute, Michio," Jakob teased, and everyone, even Michio, chuckled. Now if *I* had said that, all of them would have given me dirty looks.

"The sides of your pods will now be raised."

There was a buzz and the sides curved up and sealed above me with a gentle click. This is what it would feel like to be inside an egg. Cosy, quiet. When Jon was younger, and was heading for a meltdown, sometimes the best way to calm him would be to sit him in the pod in his room. His meltdowns were easy to trigger. All I had to do was to move his toothbrush or "accidentally" place insect repellent where he put his underarm deodorant. Not that I did that on purpose. Of course I didn't.

I glanced at the timekeeper in the curve of the cream plastic. Ten minutes to complete ten questions. Easy. Well, to be precise, as Teacher was always reminding me I should be, I now had nine minutes 57 seconds, according to the large block numbers of the timekeeper. Konstantin's experiment involved the sides of the pod heating up as we worked. Teacher stressed that we should do as many questions as we could, but as soon as we reached our pain threshold, we were to press the release button. My threshold was right on average. Five.

The first five questions were simple, but the sixth one was on physics. I hated physics. Who cares about the different types of energy anyway? Why don't they ask interesting questions, like what are the three best materials for making a cloak, or, I thought irrelevantly, should a boy have long hair?

Six minutes 32 seconds.

My pod grew hotter and I shifted my weight to distribute the heat. I couldn't even tap a desperate plea to Jakob in the next pod to beg him to tell me the answers. With the clear perspex hood down, the pod was soundproof.

In the silence, I wondered who that boy at the creek was. Why hadn't I ever seen him before?

Four minutes 32 seconds.

My pod was even hotter now. For a moment, I wished I'd worn the baggy pants favoured by most other learners. I had made this dress myself. The other girls called me weirdo under their breath, but if weirdo meant wearing something tight fitting with lacy sleeves, I was okay with that.

Beside the time, a new message glowed showing the temperature. Forty-five standards. Oh man, the sides of the pod were too hot to touch now. Why had I ever agreed to this stupid experiment? Oh, that's right, I hadn't.

My lips were dry. I would have liked a sip of creek water myself right now. I fixed my eyes on the release button. One push and I could be out of here.

Forty-nine standards.

Nothing the average desert nomad couldn't deal with. I knew that from Jakob's interest with deserts back during his second obsession, which had lasted two years. I had chosen fairy tales but although I was expected to listen to everything about sand dunes, no one expected Jakob to care about my stories of castles. I was no nomad. It was hot.

Two minutes and three seconds – and five questions to go.

If this were a fairy tale, the pod would pop open and a handsome prince, who had somehow ridden a white pony past the Evil Teacher and Vile Sir Konstantin, would lift me up behind him. He would thrust his sword into the air and cry, "Behold, I have saved you from this fate worse than death" and we would gallop off…somewhere where princes take their princesses.

That is not *logical*, as Jakob would say. I could hear him now and see the faint frown on his forehead, as he rubbed his left ear. *"How can a test designed to understand discomfort as an incentive be worse than death? You tend to..."*

"Stop it," I snapped at Jakob in my head. He will have completed the test in half the time. Michio would have been out in the first couple of minutes. I reached for the button, but then I stopped. Why should I do what other people want me to do all the time?

I decided to do an experiment of my own. I would not push the button. If I were a Zogart, no one in *my* village would starve.

I think I blacked out at fifty-six standards. Or maybe it was fifty-seven. It's important to be precise.

Mother's was the first face I saw when I woke up.

"I'm thirsty." My voice sounded raspy. She took a jug from the counter next to the examining table, and poured me a glass of water. I swallowed it down in large gulps. My right arm was encased in a soft elemental bandage. It was transparent and I could see blotches of red skin smeared in ointment. My arm must have touched the side of the pod when I passed out. I gazed around the sterile med bay.

"Second degree burns, Astatine!" Mother sighed. "They had to put you to sleep so you wouldn't feel the pain."

"I'm sorry," I said in a small voice, hoping she would hug me and tell me it was okay. There was no logical reason to break the personal space barrier, though. The wounds would heal with no scarring. The nanobots in the ointment would make sure of that. My arm was already pain-free.

"Why didn't you push the button, Astatine? You knew that this was Konstantin's pre-thesis experiment." She took the glass and placed it back on the counter. "You have ruined it by refusing to conform to standards. I have told you over and over again how important it is to behave rationally! Now he'll have to repeat the whole experiment. This may put his degree back by another month and you know how much he wanted to pass before he turns ten."

That's all Mother ever cared about. Being logical. I always thought she would love me more if I were like other children. Her job was to direct toddlers' obsessions to things useful for the community. To make me seem like the rest, I'm sure she invented obsessions for me when I was younger. I have calpics of me as a baby, sitting next to blocks lined up in a row. I'm certain that if I had that many things to build with I would have made a tower in a flash and saved my dolls from the dragons.

"Why can't he include my data, Mother?" I asked. "I'm a person too."

She refused to meet my eyes. "Of course you are. It's just that you don't always act like a regular child."

That was my mother. Straight to the point. Besides, it was true. I was not "regular," whatever that meant. I never had been.

"Have your burns been treated, Astatine?" Teacher said as he entered the med bay. He focused on my arms and did not see me.

"Yes." I pulled my arm close.

"Then leave us. I wish to speak to Susan."

Mother's real name was Daisy Sue. She's never forgiven Grandmother for calling her something so frilly, and made sure that people knew her as Susan. I'd take Daisy Sue over Astatine any day.

I went outside and sat in our car. It had its sun barrier raised, so no one could see in. I curled up in the seat, hugging my knees to my chest, and allowed myself to cry.

5

I Would Never Eavesdrop Whilst Hiding in the Cat Runs

"I've got a *burning* question for you, Zero Six," Jon said at evening meal. "How long does it take for a dumb person to know they are a pain? I mean…to know they are *in* pain."

I got up mostly so I could turn my back to him. Stupid food printer! It never quite got my taste right. I squinted hard to force the tears back. No way was I going to cry again. I placed the bowl into the left slot of the exothermer.

"Mother, Astatine is packaging her evening meal again." Jon grinned.

I made this mistake all the time, when upset. I've wrecked quite a few pieces of recyco-crockery by using the packaging function instead of the heater. I snatched it out of the compartment and placed it in the right slot just in time. In five seconds, the exothermer pinged.

I headed back to the table and tripped over Black Cat. She jumped over White Nose who lay stretched out on the floor and they both skedaddled from the room. Father likes logical names. Once he let me name a kitten, and I suggested "Puppy" to see what he would do. It was well worth it. I had never seen him use as many facial muscles in one go as then, and all to show horror. I like cats, but in my present mood, it was lucky they bolted or I probably would have given them a kick.

Still, Jon wasn't quite done. "What's wrong?" he asked. "Are you getting a bit hot under the collar?"

"Jon that is *enough*! Astatine is upset. Can't you see that she has been crying? Her eyes are red and her face is puffy."

Father and Jon examined me. I felt like a specimen in the science lab.

"Why were you crying, Zero..." Jon paused at Mother's glare, "...Astatine?"

How does one answer a question like that? It's too huge. I cried because my arm was stinging as the healing lotion wore off. Because not one person, not even I, knew why I did not obey the logical steps of Konstantin's stupid experiment. Because no one understood me, and no one ever would. Instead of answering, I did the next most logical thing. I jumped to my feet and ran to my room, almost colliding with the door which did not slide open fast enough for me.

I flung myself on my bed, planning my escape. I did this all the time. If I could, I'd be off to new adventures in a flash. The trick was getting off the island. Maybe having my eyes pop out of my head would be worth it. My calpad beeped and flashed a cally from Jon.

"May I come in?"

I checked out my room. My walls were covered with my sketches, tacked to the wall any which way. There were piles of clothes draped over my pod and a plate with a half-eaten sandwich from yesterday lay on my desk. Jon was a neat freak and wouldn't want to be in here for long. Serves him right, I thought, as I tapped a quick yes on the calpad. The door slid open and Jon hesitated, not quite game to enter.

"Mother said I had to apologise."

After a quick glance at my room, he now examined his shoes. "I think you were very brave to go beyond your pain threshold." He shifted from one leg to the other. "I know I couldn't have done it." It was true. Jon's pain threshold was almost as low as Michio's. "I am sorry that my idioms made you cry." It was useless staying mad at Jon. As much as he annoyed me at times, I knew he never said anything to hurt me on purpose.

I fiddled with a thread that had pulled in my dress. "It wasn't your fault, Jon. Things are hard for me right now. Teacher wanted to see Mother alone today. Who knows what he said? I am dreading tomorrow."

"Mother and Father are talking about that right now." Jon was reaching his limit of exposure to my mess. He turned, eager to leave.

"What do you mean?" I called after him.

Jon gestured to the calpad on the wall of my room. It was a smaller version of our family one in the kitchen. At 12:00, Mother and Father had scheduled a meeting together in the study to "discuss educational matters." It was now 12:02.

"They're talking about me!"

"That would be the logical conclusion," Jon replied as the door slid closed behind him.

As soon as he was gone, I rolled off my bed and dropped to the ground. Next to my nightstand was a grille. It took less than ten seconds to remove it. Thanks to Father's feline obsession, our house was a shrine to his cats. He promised Mother he would never keep more than five at one time, and in return, she agreed to him building elaborate cat runs all through the house. Overhead, arches where cats could climb and perch snaked and crisscrossed every room. He had built swings and heat baths, turned every table leg into a scratch post with different textures, and even placed cat elevators on the façade of the house, so the cats could reach the garden from their favourite window.

He also pulled out the linings between the walls to form hidden tunnels for them, wide enough for adventurous children. We were not supposed to play back there due to the fibre optics and cables lying around, but there was one thing that Mother and Father did not realise about me. Well, they didn't understand a lot of things about me, but there was one thing, this vital thing they did not know.

I could lie.

I did it so well that no adult ever caught me. Sometimes I felt a twinge of guilt, but it was too easy. Grown-ups were so predictable. *Everything* was so predictable that sometimes I had to lie if only to liven things up. Once I set off the Learning Hub's fire alarm system. You should have heard the howls of protest when teachers tried to herd children away from their special interests. They put it down to a faulty cable. Then there was that time I shortened Father's trousers. I was mad at him for making me try out an obsession investigation class into sewerage systems. I sniggered all through breakfast seeing the tops of his black socks that he always wore with his sandals. That was a fizzer though, as no one noticed.

I tried not to lie too often. Let's face it: lying was wrong, and unfair, because no one ever lied to me that I knew of. Yet, it was so simple! I developed this sweet, kind look and a low voice that sort of hypnotised everyone into trusting me. I could say anything I wanted, and they believed me.

No, I didn't eat the cookies.

I have no idea how White Socks became Pink Socks.

I would never eavesdrop whilst hiding in the cat runs.

It was a tight fit. I had grown a lot since I was in here last. Mother's voice was clear and agitated. I could see her feet as she paced backwards and forwards in front of the grille.

"You can't imagine what it was like, Stephen," she was saying. "She sat there covered in bandages and all I could think was 'not again!' My daughter was illogical *again*."

Yep, that's about right, I thought.

"I don't know where I went wrong," she was saying. "I did everything I could. From the age of two, I took her to every available exposure class. We've been to science labs, geology exhibitions, vehicle construction yards, but all she ever wanted to do was touch things and talk to people. I saw this coming, but I didn't want to admit it."

Father's voice was steady and low. "So what did the teacher say?"

"He sent me a spreadsheet on my calpad documenting multiple situations over several months. Astatine ticks a dozen boxes, but I don't think he has connected the dots yet. I'm sure she has it though. A mother knows."

Knows what? The cat run felt too small and claustrophobic. I started to sweat.

"Don't exaggerate, Susan. You're in no better position to judge Astatine's progress than I am, and all I see is a bright, sweet girl. Her thinking is not like most people's, but that's a good thing. We could use a bit of different around here."

"I know it's not like an illness," Mother said, "but it is something she'll have for life. There's no medicine for it, and they say it's often hereditary."

"Don't look at me." It was the first time I had heard Father snap at Mother. "It doesn't come from my side of the family!"

"Well, you are always asking people to come around here."

"To get help with my carpentry!"

Then Mother sighed. "I'm sorry. I didn't mean to accuse you. I know it's my fault. It is because of my mother."

What do they mean? There was something wrong with me, which meant I was like my grandmother, whom I adored. That didn't sound so bad.

"It's nobody's fault." Father sounded like his calm self again.

"I've done all I could. I drilled routine into her. There is not a single rule she can't quote back to me. Don't touch people. Control your emotions. Stop talking about nonsensical things. Don't invite more than two friends over at the same time. It's like she hears but it doesn't sink in."

Mother's voice faltered. Was she crying? She never cried, especially over me.

"Maybe a diagnosis wouldn't be a bad thing." Father sounded uncomfortable. "They have experts for this. They could give her de-socialisation training. What do they call them now? SoS lessons."

"People already think she is odd enough. Do you want her labelled? Parents would tell their children not to choose her as a lab partner. Nobody would include her in their thesis research, because her being different might skew the results. Do you want her to bumble her way through her own thesis, and end up with no prospect for meaningful work? No way to fit into the community?"

Why would that happen? They were scaring me now.

"Oh come on," Father coughed. "She'll do better than that. We have to keep steering her in the right direction. Sure, the sewerage system idea didn't work out, but there are other obsession investigation classes. Social Syndrome does not define who she is. She's Astatine, our wonderful daughter, that's what defines her."

The words *Social Syndrome* were thumping in my ears. Social Syndrome. *I* had Social Syndrome.

Then from the living room, I heard the sounds of trumpets. Space Seekers was starting. Nothing would keep Mother and Father from watching the latest episode. Sure enough, I heard the study door slide open and shut and I was alone.

6

Elementally We Are All the Same

I had to get away, out of the house where everyone saw me as a problem child, a potential failure. I shuffled back to my room as silently as my numbed body could manage it. In a daze, I stuffed my bed to make it look like I was sleeping there, just in case. Then I turned off the light and slipped out the window. They knew I hated Space Seekers so I was free for at least two hours, and I doubted Mother would check on me before she went to sleep.

As I rode my bike through the deserted streets, I pressed the pedals, keeping time with the rhythm in my mind. *Social. Syndrome. Social. Syndrome.* The stupid thing was I didn't even know what Social Syndrome meant. You would use those words as an insult, if someone invaded your personal space. It had to be more than that though, or else Mother and Father wouldn't be so upset. I hadn't planned it, but my feet and the rhythm in my head took me to the street where my grandmother lived. I propped the bike up against the garden shed and walked up to the door, which she had programmed to recognise me. It opened with a gentle chime.

Grandmother came out from the kitchen. "Astie Muffin. Whatever is the matter? And what happened to your arm?"

I ran to her and hugged her tight, burrowing my face into the folds of her dress, breathing in the scent of freshly printed cookies. She led me to the sofa and held my hands in hers. Space Seekers was *not* playing in the background. Grandmother hated it as much as I did.

Once I started talking, it was as if my life poured out of my mouth. About not fitting in. Not having any friends. No one understanding me. Not having a clue about my thesis. Finally, I told her about Social Syndrome. Every time I glanced at her kind crinkled face, I saw her watching me, looking me straight in the eyes. Everyone else I talked to looked at the floor or somewhere next to my left ear. When I was finished, she snuggled me close.

"Do you know what Social Syndrome is?"

"Not really," I admitted.

"This is." She gave me an extra hard hug.

"Hugs?" I said, perplexed.

"Hugs and wanting to be with people. Talking about life. Being curious about everything and obsessed about nothing."

"That doesn't seem so bad."

Grandmother brushed a stray hair from my cheek. "I don't understand myself why people are afraid of it. It has something to do with touching others and being in large groups. It's a fear that is beyond logic, which is unexpected for a community that values logic above anything else. There is nothing bad about being social, Astie, and don't you let anyone tell you different. In fact I am much that way myself."

"Yeah, Mother said that too," I agreed without thinking.

"Your mother told you that?"

"Um, I sort of hid in the cat runs and listened to Mother and Father talking about me."

"Ah. You left that bit out of your story."

"You won't tell them, will you?"

"You want me to lie for you?"

"Maybe," I said with a half-smile.

"I need a tea. How about you, Muffin?" She got up and I followed her to the kitchen where a plate of coconut cookies sat on the table. I helped myself to one and perched on a stool as Grandmother rummaged in the cupboard. I thought of our cupboard at home, with all our supplies organised alphabetically. Then a more pressing idea came to me.

"Father said something about de-socialisation training. What is it? It sounds horrible."

Grandmother's face hardened as she spooned dry mint into two mugs then filled them with boiling water from the tap. "Things have changed a lot in the past sixty years," she said as she passed me the steaming drink. "Once, anyone who behaved in a way that was not accepted by the community was seen as defective. They were either hidden away in a backroom in people's homes, or they were sent away for retraining."

I cringed at the thought. "What does retraining mean?"

"It means learning to behave in a way that allows you to fit in."

"That sounds horrible. Were you ever retrained?"

Grandmother was silent as she settled beside me and when she spoke, she sounded drained. "It was *very* important to my father that his daughter behaved appropriately. Apparently, I didn't, so they sent me to retraining when I was four years old. They dragged me out of my mother's arms and took me to a large house on the other side of the island. It was..." – she paused – "...unpleasant, but I was a *very* quick learner. I was allowed home within two months."

I tried to imagine her as a four-year-old, ripped away from everything she knew. "What did they do to you?" I whispered.

"Oh, it was not that bad, Muffin. They reminded me of the importance of manners and rules, and I have obeyed those ever since. Well, most of them."

"How come I haven't heard about this? Teacher never mentioned anything about retraining houses during our history investigation."

Grandmother sighed. "People are good at avoiding what they don't want to confront, or they get caught up in their own obsessions and ignore what doesn't affect them. As long as you are safe and fed, why should you care if a little girl goes away for a few months?"

I squirmed and picked at my bandages. Thinking about it, if half the people on my street disappeared I doubt I would notice. I rarely saw them unless they were outside working on their interests.

"People choose to forget when it is uncomfortable to remember. My parents never talked about the time that I was gone. Maybe they were ashamed of me, or afraid to admit that they had gone along with it. Most likely, Father was happy that he had obeyed protocol, and his child was no longer an embarrassment. It was as if it had never happened and everyone could live happily ever after. I got the message. I never spoke of the retraining either. That's how a whole generation can go by without being told truths of the past."

"More than one generation," I said, biting my lip.

Grandmother arched her eyebrows. "What do you mean, Astie?"

"You haven't told *me* what happened to you in retraining."

Grandmother nodded and took a sip of her tea before answering. "No, I haven't. You are right," she said. "But I'm being wise with the truth. Perhaps I will tell you when you are older. You don't have to worry about any of that, anyway. De-socialisation classes today are nothing like what I went through. They no longer take children from their families. All you have to do is go to special SoS classes for a while and learn how to behave like other people."

"What if I don't want to behave like other people?" I asked the obvious. "What if I like the way I am now?"

"Then you do what I did. Learn to pass without seeming different. Before you do or say anything, think. What would Jon do? What would your mother and father say? Pay attention to your classmates and learn to be like them. As luck would have it, those of us with Social Syndrome are good at mimicking people."

I thought about it. It wouldn't be easy, but it would be worth it.

"I can do that," I said, "I don't want de-socialisation classes. They sound bizarre."

"Yeah, bizarre is a good word for it. In a place called Elemental Island, founded by Elemental Harvesters, people should understand that elementally we are all the same. Maybe one day they will embrace the different ways those elements can be put together, but for now, tread carefully."

I reached over and gave her hand a squeeze. "Thanks, Grandmother. For everything."

She ruffled my hair. "Now, let's get those bandages off you. I can see they are irritating you." The elemental strips peeled off with ease. Grandmother examined my skin. "It's healed."

I rubbed my arm. It felt smooth and no longer tingled.

"We have to decide on what to tell your parents about tonight. Do I cally them and let them know you are with me, or do I let you sneak back home and we keep this little visit all to ourselves?"

"I vote for sneak back home."

"Okay, Muffin. Your choice. You have to go now though. It's getting late."

I stood and gulped down my tea, lukewarm by now, then gave Grandmother a big hug. She ruffled my hair and then followed me to the door. Before I stepped out into the darkness, she added, "Oh, I meant to talk to you about your thesis. I had an idea that might be perfect for it."

"Thank you, Grandmother," I said politely, trying to look interested. My thesis was the last thing I wanted to think about right now.

"I'll come round tomorrow evening to show you something. I think you'll like it."

7

The Boy Who Flew

I pedalled like a maniac. The digicast of Space Seekers had finished twenty-three minutes ago, so people wouldn't be glued to their screens anymore. Jakob said that was an illogical idiom and that he hoped no one would be glued to anything. I thought it made perfect sense, though. Have you ever seen someone obsessed with something? If you didn't see their chests move, you would swear they stopped breathing. All because of a bunch of digital aliens prancing across a screen. Sad really. Then it hit me that if I was to fit in and hide my SoS then I might have to pretend to like the show. Oh, gross!

Night-lights hidden in trees and attached to buildings made the streets appear luminescent. As all special interests were encouraged, solar power fanatics were in charge of these lights, which gave a warm and gentle glow.

A cat with a blue tail darted in front of me and before I could brake, my bike hit its side. The cat flew into the air howling in pain then limped down a gravel track that led to the beach.

"Cat!" I whispered. "I'm sorry!"

Without thought, I followed it. As I rode away from the night-lights it got darker, and I had to rely on moonlight. Luckily, there was a full moon tonight, flickering through the trees.

"Cat? Blue Tail?" I called but there was no sign of it. I couldn't bear to think of it hurt and alone. I had to find it. I got off my bike and pushed it slowly, peering into the bushes as I did. My bicycle glowed luminously, a result of Jon's early thesis work into the uses of tritium, a by-product of cold fusion.

There was no need to be afraid. No dangerous animals had been allowed when Elemental Island was populated. I certainly wasn't scared of cows, sheep and chicken, and even if I had been, they were far away in the farmlands.

All of a sudden, the bush erupted. Blue Tail darted out with an angry yowl and the next second a shadow figure lunged at me. Without thinking, I gripped its hand, bent low and used my body as a pivot to flip the figure over, face down into the sand with one arm twisted behind its back. It was easy. Martial arts training had been my chosen physical activity since I was three. "Yield?"

Close up, the full moon gave enough light to see my attacker. It was the boy with the long hair. He turned around and sat up slowly, keeping a close eye on me.

"Please do not touch me again," I said.

"Drang!" he replied, spitting sand. "You're only a girl. What sort of place is this?" He scrambled to his feet, but fell back, moaning in pain.

"Are you okay?" I took a quick look at him. He was clutching his leg and I could make out a dark patch on his right knee that had to be blood.

"Sure, just fine!"

"You don't look fine," I said, coming closer. "The shoulder throw I did can't have done that! How did you get hurt?"

He glanced up at me, his eyes locking with mine. "It's you again, from this morning," he said, slumping back with a deep sigh.

"Where did you come from?" I persisted.

"Just…leave me alone," he said. "Forget you saw me." He pulled himself up to sitting position and tried to stand. He collapsed.

I hesitated then said, "I'll go and get my grandmother. She lives close by."

"No!" he shouted. "Don't get anyone. Please," he added, pushing the last word out as if it was an effort.

Perhaps I was dreaming. This couldn't be real. I was quite sure no one had ever typed into their calpads: 14:33 Meet injured stranger on deserted beach track.

"Would you like me to check your leg?"

"You?"

I did not understand his attitude at all. All children knew first aid by the time they reached seven. By eight, I could have resuscitated a person if I had to. It was logical that every person was trained this way. The medics could take time to reach an accident, and a person could die in that time.

"Have you got a better idea?"

"Oh, this is beyond a joke," he said and raised his hands to the sky, fingers fanned out.

I had never seen people use their hands like that but he looked exasperated. I huffed.

"It is your choice!" I lifted my bike up from the ground and started to wheel it away. "I understand perfectly. You are hurt and in pain. As I am only a *girl*, I can see that I am useless to you. For your sake, I hope that your femoral artery isn't perforated or the patella cracked because, if you don't get help soon, you will never walk right again. That is," I flashed him a wry smile, "if you live."

He let me walk another ten paces, before he called feebly, "I'm sorry. Please come back."

I walked back to him. Without a word, I unclipped the med kit from under my bicycle seat, then rolled up his trousers and exposed a bloody knee. I tapped my calpad and a bright light shone around my wrist.

"What is that?" He startled and shied away from me. I glanced over my shoulder. There was nothing there.

"That!" he said again, now pointing to my hand.

"It's the torch function on my calpad." I articulated my words as if talking to an infant.

"How does it work?" he said.

I had no idea, but I was not about to confess my ignorance to someone who already thought I was useless.

"Magic," I said in a hushed voice, bringing the calpad to my chin, lighting up my face eerily in the dark. "I'm a wizard and I am going to suck your soul."

His eyes grew bigger and he backed away from me. I took pity on him.

"It's only light. It won't hurt you." I held my wrist out to him and he poked the calpad gingerly.

"Skrate," he said.

"Skrate?"

"Rad. Brill."

Although I couldn't see any injuries to his head, he was clearly babbling.

I took off my calpad and as it unfolded, the light moved to the rim so I could see the screen. I selected the Medihealth option. "How did you hurt yourself?" I asked as I waved it over the boy's knee and then read the screen.

"I slipped on a steep rock face."

"The good news is nothing is broken. The bad news is infection has already set in."

"You're just a kid. You can tell all that from that unfolding plastic thing?"

"You think I'm a goat?"

"What?"

"A kid. A baby goat?"

He laughed. "A kid is a child. A young human. Unless you are not human...?" His voice petered out.

I lifted the calpad so he could watch and so I could scan his head. "See," I said, talking slowly. "It says, '*Medical check complete.*'"

He looked at it, then back at me. "Are you the Storyteller?" He shook his head. "You can't be. You're too young for it. Are you still in training?"

"I enjoy stories, but I don't like to tell them." No one would care enough to listen, but I didn't say that.

"You know how to read though," he said, looking at me in an odd way.

"Of course I do!" To my surprise, the calpad hadn't picked up any brain anomalies, so I decided to focus on his leg. I took a lotion from my kit and smeared it all over the torn skin.

"Whoa!" he cried. I knew how he felt. It was the same lotion that had been applied to my burns...was that only this morning? It was instant pain relief. I found an elemental patch, stretched it to the right size and bandaged the wound.

"The nanobots will get rid of the bacteria, so the infection should clear in about an hour." I sneaked a quick glance at him. Strands of his long lank hair fell across his face. He was like no other boy I had ever seen.

He touched the bandage with his fingertips, and pressed harder when it didn't hurt. "How is this possible?" he whispered. "What sort of place is this?"

"What do you mean? You must have seen patches before. Where are you from? How did you get here?"

Without taking his eyes from his knee, he said, "I flew."

8

The Stranger in Shadows Who Called Me Sweetheart

I immediately checked for wings. There weren't any, of course. Birds had wings, and judging by his injury this boy was very much human.

"Flew?" I asked. "How can you fly?"

"Pa's Scouter," he replied, stretching his leg.

"What's a Scouter?"

"Ours is a Tiger Moth. What do you use?"

I pictured a large moth with a tiger's head floating in the sky. For a moment, I wondered if he had head injuries after all.

"I have no idea what you are talking about," I said.

He looked at me. "I think we have our wires crossed."

"Wires crossed? I'm not a droid. I don't have any wires. You're insane."

"Let me explain in little steps." He spoke to me in the same way I told him about the torch function on the calpad. "I flew…" he stuck his arms straight out from his body and made vroom, vroom sounds, "…a plane across the sea, and landed when I spotted this place."

It took a moment to sink in. "Is this plane a flight machine? You flew *onto* the island? From somewhere else?" My voice went up an octave with each phrase.

"Bingo!" he said. "Clever little girl."

This news was so big I did not know how to interpret it. I gaped at him as if he'd grown horns. Actually, horns would have been easier to accept. Flight was lethal. Still, this boy's eyes were in his head, and although his leg was hurt, according to Medihealth all his internal organs were intact. Besides, creating a flying machine was a thesis no one was allowed to pursue. You could dabble with the idea in your own time, and some people did, but all you could ever design was a hope machine.

I blinked hard but the impossible boy still sat before me on the ground.

"Prove it! Show me your flight…your plane?" I said, stumbling on the unfamiliar term.

"Not now. It's too dark. Besides, I'm not even sure where it is. I landed it over the hills somewhere," he waved towards the ridge. "I walked most of the day, looking for food."

"I can't believe this. Flying is impossible!" I breathed, trying to imagine what it would be like to float in the air.

The boy flexed his knee and then stood. He was not much taller than I was. "How can you heal me in minutes but not know about planes?"

"How can you fly, but not know how to fix a knee?" I retorted.

He shrugged, then smiled, showing a wide gap in his front teeth. Now I *knew* he was not from the island. Nobody here had teeth like that.

"What's your name?" he asked.

"Astie."

"Danny." He reached his hand towards me. I jumped back in alarm. Was this stranger trying to touch me?

"Sorry," he said, retracting his hand.

"I forgive you," I said without thinking. "I've never met anyone from somewhere else. I didn't even know there *were* people anywhere but here."

"Trust me, sweetheart, there's a big wide world out there. Do you have anything to eat? I'm starving."

I studied him more closely. He was dirty, but appeared well-nourished.

"You can get your own food anytime. There's a GP close by."

"GP?"

"General Printer."

I gestured for him to follow me and led him to a slab of stone about the size of a desk under a palm tree. "It's for people who want to eat on the beach."

"Sorry, but I can't eat that," he said.

I thought he was joking until I saw his face.

"Huh?" I was surprised. "Don't you make yours look like a rock or a tree? Our landscapers have a lot of rules about keeping the natural look." I tapped the side of the stone and a panel appeared. This was a simple machine with pre-programmed options, designed for people who were out and about during the day. I selected *Meal 1* and a tray slid out with a burger and a fruit juice.

"Will that do?"

I had heard the word "dumbstruck," but I had never seen anyone struck as dumb as Danny was. Perhaps flying had addled him after all.

"How…?" he began.

"I printed it. You know. 3D printing."

"It *is* magic," he whispered.

"Hardly. My cousin, Jakob, could explain it better than me, but it's got something to do with breaking a thing down to its elements to make a digital model and then use the model to create copies."

"A machine that makes food at the push of a button. I could make a fortune!"

"What does 'make a fortune' mean?"

"You know, make a lot of money."

"Money?"

"You don't have money? How do you buy things then? Or pay for someone to work for you?"

"We share our abilities and we print most things we need."

"No one will ever believe me," Danny mumbled under his breath, then took a bite of the burger. "Ah, wonderful."

Now that I could see him properly, his hair was blond and coarsely cut. The ribbon that tied it back was a rag not fit to be a cat toy. This close, I saw that the jacket he was wearing had some emblems on it and one of them had a picture of a rocket. Definitely a Space Seekers fan in the making. He backed up against the tree to eat; his grey-blue eyes darted just as our cats' did when they wanted to protect a treat from the others. Sauce smeared his lips that had the first fuzz of hair growing above them.

"Why are you here, Danny?"

"Got lost."

"Are you sure I can't get Grandmother? I know she would help you."

"No! No adults. I can't risk being found. There's no way of knowing what they do to strangers here."

"What do you mean? We *never* have strangers here."

"All the more reason not to call attention to myself." He wiped his mouth with the tissue that came with the meal. "Besides, you're a girl."

"Why do you keep saying that? What has being a girl got to do with anything?" I took the empty plate and cup from him and threw them into the recycle slot on the GP.

"You wouldn't know about these things. The people in charge wouldn't tell a girl nothing."

I laughed aloud. "Better not say that to Lena or something terrible might happen to you after all. She's our head councillor."

"You have a female leader?"

"Lots of them."

"And they make decisions for men?"

"Sure."

"Drang! I have to get off this island." He looked at me sideways. "Maybe you can help me. I need something before I can leave."

"You want me, a little girl, to help you, a big boy, to get off this nasty scary place." I was using my secret voice, the one reserved for people who annoyed me. They never understood I was being mean to them, so it wouldn't get me into trouble. Danny seemed to know exactly what I meant though.

"Okay, stop with the sarcasm," he said. "Just forget it. You've been great, Astie. Truly. I'll stay here for the night."

"You're going to sleep outside?" The thought was bizarre.

"I do it all the time when I'm scouting."

My calpad chimed a sleep warning. Unless I was in bed in twenty minutes, the home alarm would be set off. A pillow under a blanket would not fool the internal system.

"I have to go. Sorry." I paused, then added – hesitant in case he said no – "Tomorrow, do you think you could show me your plane?"

Danny did not answer at first, but then he nodded. "Okay. I have to go back anyway as I left something there I need, and maybe you can tell me about your island on the way."

"Absolutely!"

"Skrate." He slipped into the bushes, and after a couple of rustles, all was silent.

I stood on the track a moment wondering if this had all been a dream. As I pedalled home, I knew that I could not deal with this on my own. I had to tell someone, and Danny had made it clear it could not be an adult. When I got to our house, and crept back through my window, I sat on my bed and sent Jakob a cally. He would read it first thing in the morning. Luckily, it was a rest day tomorrow with no Learning Hub.

Meet Astie at the beach at 01:00.

We went to the beach together all the time. On rare occasions, I would use an excuse, like a mini obsession on shells, or studying the tide, to convince others to come with me. Except Jakob. He never needed convincing.

I lay down on my bed and stared at the ceiling. My mind churned. A flying moth with a tiger's head. A stranger in shadows who called me sweetheart. A land "out there." A tomorrow that was an unplanned adventure! When sleep came, it was vivid and restless.

9

You Have Very Long Hair for a Boy

On rest days, I would tap off my alarm and sleep in. Today, however, I leapt out of bed at 00:00. I was going to see the plane! Would Danny still be there this morning? He had to be!

I shoved a med kit and a mini toolkit into my backpack. I added some of Jon's spare clothes from the pile he kept in the hallway closet, including the shirt Grandmother printed him for his birthday. I knew he wouldn't miss them. He had two sets of favourite clothes that he alternated on washdays. Then I went to the kitchen and programmed the food printer for a picnic lunch. There was no GP where we were going.

Mother came in at 00:20. "What are you doing, Astatine?"

"Jakob and I are going to the beach," I explained as I grabbed three bananas. Fresh fruit always tasted better than printed ones.

She crossed her arms on her chest. "I'm sorry, you can't!"

I paused, banana in hand. "Why not?"

She pointed to the calpad on the wall. My heart sank. I had forgotten our outing to the cold fusion plant. Since tritium was a by-product of cold fusion, it was plentiful. Although finding new uses for it was not as glamorous as inventing hover boots, Jon's thesis was eagerly awaited. He made frequent trips to the power plant to delve into the practical applications of his research and I was expected to support him.

I hated how impressive Jon's thesis sounded. To make myself feel better, I thought of the reminder chart he still used every day, even at fourteen. I gave mine up at five. Honestly, who needs a calpic of a toothbrush to use one, or of shoes to remember to put on a pair? Mother was very proud when I deleted my chart so young. I'm not the best in my family at too many things, but being organised is one of them. I am also the best at getting bored. No chance of that today though, as long as I could get out of touring the factory again.

I was about to complain when I remembered Grandmother's words. What would Mother do? To her, a change in the timetable would be the most upsetting factor. Now was a good time to start creating the new me.

"I hadn't forgotten, Mother and I am disappointed I'm not able to accompany you to the factory. Jakob needs my help to gather samples of the sand at the beach, for his research into seasonal changes in the composition of seawater. It was decided yesterday and I feel it is my duty to assist my cousin."

I showed her the appointment on my calpad. "I regret that I did not update the family calpad. Does this cause you concern?"

Mother glanced in my direction, puzzled, and then she *looked* at me. Her mouth opened and shut a couple of times, then she said, "I am not concerned. We will not be back until 10:45. I presume you'll be back by then?"

I nodded and typed a cally for Jakob. "Schedule update: return before 10:45."

I got an immediate reply. "Already scheduled SP at 09:30."

I bit my lip. If we had to be back by 09:30 for his Sensory Park session, would we have enough time to get to the plane and back?

I arrived at the beach a few minutes before 01:00, out of breath, my hair sticky with sweat from the back of my neck. To my dismay, there were people there already. A couple walked their dog and a family was spraying their sandcastle with liquid glass, ready to take it home.

I heard an unfamiliar whistle coming from somewhere close to me and knew right away that this was no bird. I made sure no one was watching me, before ducking behind the bushes. Danny was crouched beside a boulder with the blue-tailed cat curling around his legs.

"I see you made a friend," I said.

"I think she adopted me," Danny replied, and stroked her head. "Poor thing's got paint on her. I can't get it off."

The bushes parted and the cat scampered away as Jakob entered the grove.

"What are you doing in here, Astie?" Spotting Danny, he focused on the ground. "Good morning," he said, obeying the greeting protocol in a monotone. "My name is Jakob. You have very long hair for a boy."

"Jakob, this is Danny."

"What's this guy doing here?" Danny hissed. "I asked you not to tell no one."

"You said no adults, but Jakob is the same age I am."

Danny shuffled out of the thick part of the bush and brushed twigs off his jacket as he stood up. "Girls are no good at keeping secrets."

"What secrets?" Jakob's eyes were still fixed on the ground.

Danny laughed in a way that seemed unkind. "You talking to an ant?"

"*He's* being polite and not staring at you," I said in Jakob's defence.

"Your teeth are crooked and you have halitosis," Jakob observed with his peripheral vision. "Your nose appears to have been broken and reset and your bathing patterns need rescheduling. Who are you? Where are you from?"

"Huh," Danny snorted. "Quite the charmer, aren't you?" He turned to me. "Do you have anything to drink? There are too many people around for me to get to the creek and I'm dying of thirst."

"You exaggerate a lot," I observed. "Where's your flask?"

Danny took it from his backpack and held it out. I poured water from my bottle, careful to make sure the two mouthpieces didn't touch. He drained it in a couple of gulps.

"If you need more there's always a Skywater vessel close by," I said. I pulled some branches aside. "There's one."

Danny came up beside me and our shoulders brushed. It was very rude of him and I moved away, but I don't think he noticed. One of the dog walkers came up, turned on a tap, and let his puppy drink from the stream of water.

Danny scratched his head. "That thing that's shaped like a big pineapple is a water tank?"

"It's not a tank. Well, it is sort of, but it doesn't collect rainwater. It makes water from the air. Don't you have them where you come from?"

"Never seen one before."

"But they're everywhere." Jakob's forehead furrowed.

Danny ignored him. "How does it work?"

"Um..." I tried to think back to science lessons. "Something to do with soaking up humidity from the atmosphere."

"Adiabatic distillation," Jakob said, as if stating the obvious.

"Did your Engineer make that?"

"No," I laughed. "Jakob's ancestor on his mother's side designed it over a hundred years ago."

"Your ancestor was the Engineer?"

"The Engineer?" Jakob echoed. "What a peculiar thing to say. She was an industrial scientist."

"And today, nobody makes them. We print them on the GPs. Like the one we used to print your food last night."

"So you '*print*' everything you need!"

"Well, not everything. Sometimes there are things that are too complex for the home printer so then you order them."

"Without paying?" he asked, his voice going high pitched in excitement. "I've heard the Storyteller talk about things like this. Can you press on a picture of what you want and then it is delivered to you?"

"Yeah, it has an ordering function," I answered, talking about the calpad.

"And if your device does not work, does your Engineer fix it?"

"Sort of…" I began, but Jakob interrupted. "Astatine," he demanded, "these are infantile questions. Who is this person and where does he come from?"

Danny looked at me. "Can I trust him? Will he tell anyone that I am here?"

"Why are you talking as if I can't hear you?" Jakob sounded annoyed.

I lowered my voice to a whisper. "Danny is not from the island. He *flew* here in a pla…I mean a flight machine!"

Jakob shook his head. "Not possible. He is alive."

"You can tell?" Danny said. "Is it my breathing that gives me away? I've tried to give it up, but it's sort of addictive."

"It *is* possible. Look at him. Have you ever seen clothes like that?"

"No." He didn't look at Danny. Jakob had a photographic memory, so I knew he had noticed every detail of Danny's jacket the minute he set eyes on him. "What does N A S A mean?" he asked, spelling out the letters.

"What's N A S A?" Danny was confused.

"He is talking about the markings on that emblem," I said, pointing to Danny's chest.

"Well then, why doesn't he say that?" He turned to Jakob. "No idea, brah. Lots of things have those markings on them."

"May I observe more closely?" Jakob held out his hand.

Danny backed away. "The bomber jacket's been in our family for years. I am not going to gift it to you, no matter how much you want it."

"I do not want to confiscate your attire. I wish to observe it for its protective qualities."

"What is he talking about?"

"He wants to see if it is the jacket that has let you fly without being harmed," I explained.

Danny paused a moment, then slipped it off and gave it to Jakob. "There's nothing magical about it. The only thing it protects me from is the cold."

Jakob turned the jacket inside out and back before returning it. "It is an ordinary jacket, with no special protective qualities."

"This guy's a genius." Danny put the jacket back on.

Jakob bit his lip in concentration then without looking at Danny, he asked, "So, you came in a flight machine? From off Elemental Island?"

"Is that what this place is called? Yeah, I flew here from the mainland."

Jakob began to rock where he stood. That was not a good sign.

"Jakob," I said. "What's wrong?"

10

Code Red One

The rocking became jerky. "It is forbidden," Jakob spoke in a staccato voice. "You are a stranger. Code Red One."

I recognised the term from the community rulebook, but couldn't quite place it. "What is Code Red One?" I asked quietly, to soothe him.

"Report stranger immediately. Imminent danger of contagion." He began to flap his hands in agitation.

"What is he talking about?" Danny grabbed my arm, and then let go right away. "Is he going to report me?"

"1.1.1 Infection Prevention (IP) must be notified immediately." Jakob was reciting the rulebook from memory. *"1.1.2 Avoid all contact with suspect."* His eyes grew wide. "He touched you! *2.3.1 You must go into isolation immediately!*"

"Jakob, stop it! Look!" I pulled up the health check I had done on Danny and handed the calpad to Jakob. As he studied the data, his breathing grew calmer.

"You are not contagious," he said at last. "However you have a zinc deficiency which would account for your stunted growth, your acne and the poor condition of your hair and nails. I also suspect you may be mentally deficient with inferior reproductive organs." He took a deep breath. "The latter means you may not be able to reproduce which could be a side benefit to the human population."

Danny squinted at him. "Did you say I had stunted growth?"

Jakob gave a slight grin. "Speculation confirmed." He handed the calpad back to me. "This boy is not a health hazard."

"I told you so. And Jakob," I added breathlessly, "Danny's taking me to see his flight machine. Do you want to come too?"

Danny snorted in surprise, but I ignored him.

Jakob wrinkled his forehead, rubbing his ear. "I would like to observe the machine, but..."

I didn't let him finish. "Right, that's settled then," I said. I pulled Jon's clothes out of my pack and gave them to Danny. "Put these on. They should fit you if you roll up the arms and legs. Make sure you tuck your hair up into the cap."

Danny slipped off his jacket and reached up to unbutton his shirt, but stopped as he saw the horror on our faces.

"What did I do now?"

"You are undressing!" I squeaked.

He ran his fingers through his hair, as if he wanted to pull at the roots. "That's what you told me to do, sweetheart."

"Wait until we leave." Jakob and I almost fell out of the bushes in our haste.

"This place is crazy," I heard Danny mumble under his breath.

The glare from the sand was blinding for an instant until the nano-coating on my eyes adjusted. The sandcastle family was gone and waves whooshed and sucked softly on the shore. Everything was deceptively peaceful.

"Why did you invite me to come, Astie?" Jakob asked when we were out of earshot. "You know we should report him, contagious or not."

That was why Jakob was not just my cousin but also my best friend. He didn't always understand why I broke rules, but he always asked me first before getting me into trouble.

"We can report him later, Jakob. Please, let's see the flight machine first. Once the scientists get hold of it, it might be locked away for years while they study it!" I didn't want to think of what they'd do to Danny.

"You could have gone with that boy to see this machine without telling me."

"Danny said he left it in the meadows. He must have been lucky to avoid the droids that herd the cattle, but I doubt we can do that a second time."

Jakob understood me right away. "You want me there in case the Overseer turns up to investigate. To wipe its memory so you are not caught. Astie, I was eight when I last did that. Besides, it wasn't against the rules that time, because it was training."

"There is no rule that states, 'You shall not catch a robot and wipe its memory.'"

"There is a rule that states, 'Do not interfere with robots.' Besides, perhaps the scientists *should* be the first to investigate."

"I know, Jakob, but if you get a chance to see a real flying machine up close, maybe you could adapt it for your thesis!"

Jakob was eight when he registered reverse electromagnetism as his twelve-year-old thesis. He had not changed his mind since.

"Even if I could, flying is *forbidden*, Astie. I have no wish to spend my life designing a hope machine."

"It's forbidden because people think it will harm you. We know Danny flew without coming to harm.

For today, let's just go and look. You know you want to. Be adventurous for once! We can think about rules later."

I held my breath until he gave the barest nod and then I did a small celebratory dance inside my head as Danny emerged from the bushes.

He was wearing Jon's clothes and cap. Luckily, with the pants so long, no one would notice that his own shoes had laces. "I look like a right twerp," he said, trying to tuck in the shirt.

"You fit in and that's the main thing. Now let's get going," I said, before Jakob could change his mind.

"Did you bring anything to eat?" Danny asked as we walked. "I'm starved."

I reached into my backpack and handed him an exothermal bag with a sandwich that I'd printed in the morning. "It's cheese, so you can heat it up if you like."

"Huh?" Danny held the bag as if it was going to explode.

"Do you want your cheese melted?" He gulped and nodded. I took it from him and pressed the small button on the front. I could feel the bag expanding as the food inside heated up. "There, it's ready." I handed it back. Danny opened it gingerly and took out the hot sandwich, shaking his head.

We hadn't gone far before I heard a meow. Turning, I spotted Blue Tail following us.

"There are no rats here, kitty," Danny called out to her. "You're out of luck."

Blue Tail came close and rubbed up against his leg, purring. "I'm a regular cat magnet," he mumbled.

Jakob pursed his lips. "Perhaps if you washed more often, the attraction would diminish."

Danny bent down to pet the cat. "You'll have to toughen up, buddy, or you'll end up on someone's plate."

The thought made the hairs on my arm bristle.

"You're kidding, right?" I said, hoping it was all a joke. "No one would eat a cat!"

Danny shrugged. "*We* wouldn't eat them 'cause Pa likes that they catch rats, but there are plenty others who would. If they were hungry enough."

I tried not to think about it. "Father lives for his cats," I said. "They'd never catch a rat though. Doubt they would know how."

We walked on, Blue Tail falling in step with Danny. There were two ways to get to the meadows. We could walk down the coastal road, but that would take longer and people would spot us. Logically, that shouldn't be a problem. Seeing someone you didn't know was common. Most people kept to themselves and had a small circle of friends, from the Learning

Hub of their childhood, or people who shared their obsession. Danny looked out of place though. It was hard to say why, but even how he walked made him look different. He swung his arms in an uncontrolled way. Plus if he took off the cap, we could never explain the hair.

To avoid people we took the second option, setting out to walk the inland route up and over the volcanic ridge. Once off the main path, the surface was uneven, and I kept my eyes on my boots in an attempt to concentrate. I didn't want to stumble in front of Danny. The path was steep, and my legs began to ache with the unfamiliar exercise. Blue Tail followed for a short time, then with her tail high, sauntered back into the bushes. Wise cat.

"Let me take your pack," Danny said after a while, trying to slip it off my shoulder. "It's too heavy for you."

"How could you know that?" Jakob asked. "You don't know how heavy it is, or Astie's capacity for weight bearing."

Danny raised his hands. "Drang! I was trying to be helpful. Carry it yourself for all I care." He forged ahead until he reached an almost vertical rock face.

"I think this is where I slipped and hurt my knee," he commented.

I sighed. Climbing wasn't my thing, but there was no other way. I started up, grabbing at any root I could find. They were easier to hold than the sharp edges of the black rocks. Jakob was all legs and arms, no grip. Pebbles rolled down in our wake. Danny clambered up with ease, and was the first one to reach the top. He watched as Jakob slid back a few times before reaching the crest.

"I guess 'stunted growth' can come in handy after all," Danny smirked.

I sat down wiping the sweat from my face with the sleeve of my T-shirt. No lace today, I had come prepared. Beneath us, the perfectly gridded town was toy-sized.

Danny turned to continue down the other side and stopped dead.

"Whoa!" he exclaimed. "What's that?" Far below on the other side of the ridge was a grassy knoll with dozens of mottled white and brown cows.

"It's the meadow you came from yesterday, isn't it?" I replied.

"No. That!" He pointed. On the horizon was the silhouette of the factory district.

"Those are the factories. The ones where we desalinate water and process food."

"Desali...what?"

"Take salt out of the water."

"So you can drink it?"

"Yeah."

"Desalination is a process..." Jakob began, but Danny cut him off.

"Back home, whenever there's no water, people die. We can't drink seawater."

"That's horrible."

He gestured to the factories. "Is that where your Engineer works?"

"Not exactly," I laughed, thinking of some of the engineers I knew. "Anyway, the factories are worked by droids."

"Droids?" Danny asked, still staring at the horizon.

"Automatons. Sometimes people do go there and check things are working okay, but mostly the Overseers gather data then send reports each week to a real person. They also send an alarm if there is a problem."

"This real person – is he the Engineer?"

"No. He or she would be an administrative person. Do you have an obsession with engineering?"

Danny paused before answering. "You could say that."

"She did say that," Jakob noted.

"Do you want to meet an engineer?" I offered. "Any particular specialisation? Civil, electrical, mechanical, bio-molecular, environmental, electronic?"

Danny let out a long, sharp whistle. "This is insane," he said. "You have more than one Engineer? Do you know any who can work computers?"

"I know dozens. Most children do some form of computer engineering as one of their obsessions. Jakob has a degree in the basics."

Danny spun to face Jakob. "*You* are a computer engineer?"

A strange look I had never seen before passed over his face. It was almost a smile, but his eyes squinted. I did not like it.

11

Fear of Butterflies Is Surprisingly Common

It took ages to trek down the far side of the ridge and reach the meadows dotted with tiny blue flowers. I had forgotten how good wildflowers smelled. I picked a bright pink one from a low shrub and took a whiff. Danny was watching me, so I lifted it close to his nose.

"I can't smell nothing," he muttered.

"That would be the zinc deficiency I was talking about," said Jakob. "Frangipani is in fact one of the most fragrant flowers."

"Where is your plane?" I asked.

Danny shielded his eyes as he scanned the grass. "I landed at dusk and I didn't want the Scouter to be out in the open when the sun came up. Pa is manic about keeping it in the shade. Sunlight is the Scouter's worst enemy. I aimed for the flattest bit of grass I could find and then taxied to some trees."

"Taxied? What does that mean?"

"I drove along the ground."

"It's possible to drive a flight machine?" Jakob asked.

"Sure. How do you think it flies? It's got to drive fast over the land before it takes off."

"Really! I thought it would lift straight off the ground."

"That's stupid," Danny said.

"There are some trees over there." I gestured towards a small patch of woods.

"Yeah, that could be the spot. Let's head that way for now."

All of a sudden, he yelped and flapped his hands in the air.

From fine to meltdown in 0.01 seconds. Even Jon couldn't beat that. "What's wrong?" I asked.

"Butterfly!" he croaked. A pale yellow insect wafted in the breeze.

"Lepidopterophobia," Jakob said with a shrug.

"What?" I asked, bewildered by both the boys.

"Fear of butterflies," Jakob explained as he reached out and allowed the butterfly to land on his hand. "It's surprisingly common."

Danny started to hyperventilate.

"Get rid of it, Jakob. You're frightening him."

Jakob flicked his hand and the butterfly fluttered away towards the ridge.

"I don't understand," I said. "How can you be afraid of a little thing like that?"

"Everyone is! They make you sick."

"Not here, they don't." I could tell he didn't believe me.

Jakob read his calpad. "It's 04:00 already. We'd better hurry."

"Zero four hundred?" Danny repeated as we picked up our pace. "But it's daylight?"

"Yes." Seeing his confusion I added, "You know. It's four hours after rising time."

"For us zero four hundred is four hours after midnight."

Jakob huffed. "That is illogical. The day starts when you rise. I am beginning to surmise that you live in a very strange world."

"Now that's the pot calling the kettle black, brah."

We kept walking and neither Jakob nor I were game to ask what he meant.

A calf wandered up to us, staying just out of patting reach. It was a cute little thing with a mottled brown and white face. A large cow nearby glared at us, protective of her baby.

"What do you call a cow that plays a musical instrument?" Danny said out of nowhere.

"Bovines cannot play instruments," Jakob said.

"A moo-sician."

It took me a moment to understand him, then I giggled.

"What do you call a cow that gives no milk?"

"What?"

"An udder failure!"

I understood that one straight away and burst into laughter. I had never heard words used like this before.

"Why are you laughing?" Jakob asked me. "He is talking nonsense."

"I guess he *cown't* understand us," Danny guffawed. "Maybe we'd *butter* stop."

All of a sudden, Jakob fell to the ground and hissed, "Droid!"

My laughter vanished and I dropped to the grass. "Get down," I whispered to Danny. He obeyed instantly.

A machine shaped like a large dog came bouncing over the meadow on four spindly legs. It emitted a slight whirr as it navigated the bumps in the terrain with ease. A cylindrical sensor spun around where the dog's head should have been. The cattle ignored it and kept munching the grass.

"Wha...what is that?!" Danny stammered.

"It's a cattle droid," Jakob said. "It is checking the herd to make sure the cows are healthy and unharmed."

"You mean you have cows that are armed?" Danny looked scared.

Jakob rolled his eyes. "Cattle don't have arms. They have legs and hooves."

"No, I mean what kind of weapons do they have?"

"Astie, your friend is talking nonsense again."

I laughed. "*Unharmed*, Danny. Not unarmed."

He started snickering. "Imagine a whole herd of them with guns. The *steaks* would be very high."

I smothered another wave of laughter as the droid rumbled closer. It waggled its antennae in our direction, making whizzing sounds, turned and headed across the field. We waited until it was out of sight.

"What's wrong with you two?" Jakob pressed his lips together as he stood and brushed the grass off his clothes. "We could have avoided detection if you had been silent. Let's hope it didn't file the data as suspicious. If it did, then things may become very complicated." He turned to Danny. "Where is your flight machine? The sooner we see it then the sooner we can get out of here."

"There!"

In the distance, I caught a glint of light in a cluster of trees. As we drew closer, Jakob and I slowed until we both stood stunned, gaping at the machine. A long fat tube sat on an angle with one end on the ground and the other resting on struts with wheels. Two panels jutted out from each side. In the centre of the tube were two large holes for people to sit.

"Ain't she a beauty? She's the best Scouter around."

"It's open to the elements!" I exclaimed. "There's no roof. How do you breathe?"

"Through my nose."

"What prevents your internal organs from exploding?" Jakob asked.

"I don't eat beans before I fly?"

I had seen flight machines before. Our family attended every unveiling. The first one I ever went to was for the hope machine in the Beach Park. Some were round balls relying on harnessing antigravity to create lift. Some had spinning discs on top designed to propel the machine into the air. Others were tubes shaped like this machine and even had the panels that stuck out either side like this one did. They were all similar in one aspect though. They enclosed the driver in layers of protection. "Where are all your protective devices?" I asked.

"It's got seatbelts," Danny shrugged. "They're handy if you want to fly upside down."

"Upside down!" I squeaked. "Why would you do that?"

"It's fun! But best if Pa doesn't catch me doing it though."

I went closer and ran my fingers over the bright yellow body of the machine. It was hard and smooth. "What's it made of?"

"That bit is plywood," Danny explained, "with many layers of varnish."

Jakob had gotten over his initial shock and came up next to me. "Plywood makes sense. It would be light, but strong." He rubbed one of the wide panels that stuck out above and below the body on each side.

"That part of the wing you are touching is linen."

"They're called wings?" I smiled. "I guess that's a good name for them, although I have never seen a moth with wings on top of each other."

I went to the back of the machine. There were three smaller wings, one upright and two either side. The upright one was painted in a pattern that coiled into the face of a snarling cat. It was nothing like the ones we owned though. It seemed fierce and dangerous.

"What are these?" I asked.

"That's the rudder, or the tail. It directs where the plane goes."

"Does it wag its tail when it's flying?" The thought was too funny.

"Not unless it's happy."

I giggled. I can't remember a day that I had laughed this much – ever. The muscles in my jaw ached.

"Inanimate objects do not have emotions," Jakob remarked.

Danny shook his head. "Don't you ever get a joke?"

"Of course I do," Jakob replied as he moved to the front of the plane. "It's called humour, and I am considered a very humorous person. Where's the cold fusion mechanism?"

"The cold what?"

"Cold fusion."

"Well, it can get pretty cold once you're flying, that's why I wear the jacket, and your butt can get fused to the seat..."

"You don't know what cold fusion is?" Even I was surprised at that. Everything in our community ran on cold fusion. What else was there?

"What fuels this machine then?" Jakob asked.

"Gasoline." Danny pointed to a tank set into the top wing above where people sat. Then he reached past Jakob to lift up a panel in the side of the plane, exposing the engine.

Jakob skipped with excitement. "It's so primitive! So many things can go wrong with a machine like this. It's amazing it flies at all."

"Tell me about it!"

"I *am* telling you," Jakob replied. "You must be very brave to trust your life to something that is fuelled by flammable liquids."

"Ah, thanks." Danny didn't seem sure whether he'd been insulted.

"So why did you come to Elemental Island?" Jakob asked. "This machine does not look safe to fly such long distances."

His eyes flickered away, before he answered. "I, ah, got lost. My compass and my map fell from the Scouter."

Compass? Why did that seem familiar? Then I remembered.

12

In the Air It Looks Like a Great Big Moth

"You dented Neil's mower!" I cried.

"No, I didn't," he said a little too quickly. "I don't even know any Neil."

"When the compass dropped from your flight machine, it landed on a mower. The compass is shattered, by the way. I guess the scarf is yours as well?"

"What scarf?" Jakob asked.

"You have it?" Danny sounded relieved.

I opened my pack and pulled out the scarf. Danny grabbed it. "Skrate! It flew off my neck as I came in for landing. I dropped the compass trying to catch it. Almost fell out of the plane too. Pa would kill me if I lost that." Seeing the look of horror on our faces he added, "Well, not *actually* kill me. I'd get into heaps of trouble, though. My Granny made it for my Grandpops, so he'd always know his way home. It's the best map around."

"Perfect," I said, mulling this over. "Now you have your map back, and we can print you a new compass. Jakob and I got to see a plane, and now you can go home and we won't have to report you!"

"Ah, yeah. That would be great. Get me a compass and I'm outta here," Danny said. I started to relax but then he added, "And some fuel, obviously."

"Fuel? This type of fuel is not in use anymore," Jakob said. "I don't even know if there's any on the island."

"Bother," Danny replied, but did not look bothered at all. "No fuel, no fly."

"Wait," I said, "What about the generators at the factories? We saw them on the Learning Hub visit last year. They were backups used before cold fusion. They would have used gasoline, right? I bet there are still supplies around somewhere."

Jakob nodded. "But how could we get it? We can't walk in and ask for it."

"I'll think of something." I tried to sound confident. "Maybe I could pretend to have a mini obsession. Father would take me there in flash."

"Perhaps. You will have to do it tomorrow. Danny has to leave before he is discovered."

"No problem." My mind was frantically working on how to steal obsolete fuel without anyone noticing.

"Skrate," Danny smiled, showing the gap in his teeth.

Jakob turned back to the plane and switched right back to obsession mode. "So how does the engine start?"

"See, those are the connection terminals and these cables go to the prop."

"Prop?"

"Propeller. That big thing at the front. My Grandpops made that one himself out of maple. It's got fifteen layers of resin."

"That would have taken ages. Why didn't he just print one…?" I stopped. "Oh…"

"Yeah, you got it. When you can't print things whenever you want them, sweetheart, then someone has to make things. It takes heaps of time just to keep the Scouter going. You know she's almost two hundred years old. Of course, each individual piece of her is quite a bit younger and is replaced as needed."

"Two hundred years!" The number was mind-boggling. "We recycle everything so nothing is ever old."

Danny stroked the side of the machine as Father would stroke his cats. "The Tiger Moth keeps us alive, so we have to keep her alive."

"Tiger Moth? Why is it called that?" Jakob asked.

"Dunno. I guess when it's in the air it looks like a great big moth."

"How does the propeller start?" Jakob got back to facts.

"When you crank it, it spins round and round which starts the magneto which sends a spark to ignite the fuel in the engine."

"So the start mechanism is based on magnets? That's positively attractive."

Danny laughed. "You *do* have a sense of humour."

"I wouldn't like you to think negatively of me." Jakob gave a small grin.

"What are you guys talking about?" I asked.

"Don't get charged up. It's nothing a girl would understand," Danny said.

Boys! First, they hate each other and then they are best friends.

"Can I sit in it?" I asked.

"Sure, but don't touch anything," Danny replied. "Stand on there and hoist yourself into the cockpit."

I climbed up and looked down into the seat area at the front of the plane. "There are no cocks. Why is it called a cockpit?"

"Do you always ask so many questions? Besides, the cockpit is at the back. That's the passenger seat at the front."

I reached down to the seat and lifted up a curious object that was lying in the middle of a coil of rope. It had two bracelets that could open and shut, joined by a small chain. "What's this?" I asked.

Danny bit his lip. "Ah, nothing much," he said, "They are for keeping you safe when you fly. You, um, link one end to a lever and the other to your wrist, so you do not, ah, get tossed around if the plane gets buffeted too much."

He's making it up as he goes along! I thought to myself. Why would he lie about this?

"Try the pilot's seat," Danny suggested. "You get a better feel for how to fly."

"What's a pilot?" I asked.

"I am. I pilot the plane. You know, fly it."

I slid myself into the narrow space. There was just enough room to sit and stretch my legs a little. At first, the smell was overpowering. Oil, fuel, dirt, and I hated to think of the centuries of body odour that had seeped into the grubby cloth seats. I breathed through my mouth and studied the numerous dials and levers in front of me. Starter. Park Break. Primer. Exotic language for a boy who couldn't read. I shut my eyes and imagined lifting off the ground and hovering over Elemental Island.

Danny leapt up onto the wing and stood above me.

"How did you learn it?" I asked.

"Pa taught me. He is the Scout. I'll be the Scout one day."

"Scout?" I echoed.

"We look for things from the air. Things the town needs. Sometimes we land and grab them. Sometimes we direct the Foragers where to look."

His world could be a Zogart village for all that I understood.

"How do you see where you are going?" I asked.

"Lean over the edge," Danny answered.

"Ughh," I groaned as I pushed myself up, trying to see around the body of the plane. "I think this design needs a major overhaul."

"I sit on a parachute to give me a bit more height," Danny confessed.

"What's a parachute?" I asked.

"More questions! It's what you strap onto your back if you want to jump out of a plane. It opens up like a big sheet to slow your fall."

"You jump out of a plane while it's in the sky? You'd die!"

"That's what the parachute is for, sweetheart," Danny shrugged. "So you *don't* die."

By now, Jakob was also on the wing peering into the cockpit. He grabbed some fat padded earphones and put them on his head. "Nice," he said, as he took them off again. "I wear earphones all the time too. Do you have sound sensitivities?"

"I don't know about sensitivities but it gets loud up there," Danny said.

What could be noisy in the sky? Birds?

Jakob caught on first. "Ah! Fuel engines would be noisy. Cold fusion is silent."

"A *hover* flight machine would be silent too," I said to him. "Wouldn't it be amazing if this could fly using inverse electricmagnetism?"

"Reverse electromagnetism," Jakob corrected me.

"What are you two talking about?" Danny asked.

"Jakob's thesis is going to be on a hope machine that floats in the air..." I was going to say using electromagnetism, but knew he would not understand, so continued, "...by magic, without fuel."

"What's a hope machine?"

"It's when you spend many years designing something according to all the known rules of science but you can't make it because it's too dangerous or the materials are not available."

"So let me get this right, some of you spend a lot of time..."

"At least six years," I added. "Sometimes a lifetime."

"...designing something impossible to make."

"Yeah. That's right."

"That's dumb!"

I laughed, "Yes! I agree." Catching the grimace on Jakob's face, I added, "But there have been some amazing inventions that started as hope machines and worked in the end. Jakob's father invented boots that make you float in the air."

"Get out of here!"

I was shocked at his rudeness, but he was smiling, which made no sense at all.

"Get out of where?" Jakob asked in his monotone.

"Drang, you guys are so strait-laced. I meant, wow, floating boots! That's amazing!"

"Yes," Jakob agreed. "Father's invention is inspirational. People thought it could not be done, and he proved it otherwise."

"Riiiight." Danny dragged out the word. I could almost hear the thoughts churning in his brain. "And you want to design a 'flight' machine that floats in the air in the same way."

"Correct."

"Good idea, brah," Danny said as he slapped Jakob on the back.

In an instant, he was on his knees on the wing with his arm twisted in the air. Jakob stood over him with a blank face. "Yield," he said calmly.

"I yield! I yield!" Danny whimpered and then rubbed his arm as Jakob let go. "What did you do that for?" he demanded as he got to his feet.

"You attacked him," I said. "What did you expect?"

"I didn't *attack* him. I slapped him on the back. Where I come from, that's what friends do."

I tried to imagine a place where people hit each other for fun.

"It seems to me that all your people have a severe case of Social Syndrome," Jakob said.

I stiffened. I had thought the same thing, but wasn't game to say it. Besides, a whole world full of socials sounded wonderful.

"A bad case of what?" Danny asked.

"Ignore, him," I said. "He's being a repulse."

"So how does this fly?" Jakob's eyes scanned the cockpit.

"I could take you for a short flight," Danny said. The blood rushed to my head and my palms began to sweat. Flying would be a dream come true! Then I realised that Danny was talking to Jakob. He had the same strange expression I noticed on his face before –

that squinty half smile. He was up to something but I had no idea what.

Jakob shook his head. "No, thank you," he said. "It is forbidden. Astie will locate the fuel for you, and then you must leave."

"I can't believe you'd give up this chance," I exclaimed. "I'll go! Take me!"

"It's too late," Jakob said, pointing.

13

How to Immobilise an Overseer without Sheep-Tackling Experience

Striding across the meadow, squashing dozens of blue flowers with its oversized feet, came the Overseer. Like all others of its type, it was humanoid. This one was female with short black hair. The dog droid must have notified her after all.

"Do you know this series?" I whispered to Jakob. "Can you wipe her memory?"

"I'm not sure. I was only allowed to work on the old ones when I was in training." He peered at the approaching Overseer. "She's a 300 model. I should be able to do this."

"What *is* that?" Danny squeaked.

"She's a robot. The droids feed data to her and then she investigates anything out of the ordinary.

If she decides we are a threat to the cattle, she will alert the controller. Otherwise she will include it in the data sent at the end of the week."

"My plane is out of the ordinary. And it's been here since yesterday. Maybe she's already reported it!"

"If that were the case," Jakob said as if talking to a child, "your 'plane' would be surrounded by Monitors by now."

"What are Monitors?"

"They keep the community secure and deal with issues."

"Ah. We call them Sheriffs. Don't want to get on *their* bad side."

"That would be right." Jakob turned back to the robot. "Her criteria for investigation must be very specific. If it is not an immediate threat to the cows then it won't be reported early. Luckily, *I* didn't program her, or you would be in quarantine already."

"Huh," Danny snorted. "Think you're smart, do you?"

"I am smart."

"Yeah, he is," I agreed.

"So what's the plan?"

"We have to immobilise her first. Then I can get to the panel on her chest."

"Do you want me to tackle her?" Danny flexed his muscles. "I've downed a few sheep in my time."

"Why would you tackle sheep?"

"We used to cross them with cattle, but all we got were animals in a baaaaahd mooood."

I burst out laughing.

Jakob frowned then said, "Yes."

"Yes what?"

"Yes, I want you to tackle her."

I shot him a look, but said nothing. This was shaping up to be one of the best days I had ever had.

As the Overseer drew closer, I could see her fixed pleasant features and her model number, 306, on the black and white casing that covered her chest.

"She's got slanty eyes." Danny sounded surprised.

"Her face and hands are humanoid. Made to look like her designer's," I explained.

"A girl made that? A girl with slanty eyes?"

I frowned at his attitude. "Derogatory comments about someone's appearance are impolite." I sounded like my mother, which was unexpected. "You should have no problems tackling her. After all, she's only a girl robot, made by a slanty-eyed woman."

I thought I saw Jakob smile, although it might have been a trick of the light.

By the time we got down from the plane, she had reached us, bouncing over boulders and cowpats.

"You are unauthorised. Please state your purpose?" She had a gentle voice.

"Greetings, 306," I said, polite as can be. "We are standing in front of a forbidden flight machine flown here by a stranger who's going to bring you down like a sheep."

Jakob actually laughed at something I said. It felt good.

"What did you say that for!?" Danny spluttered.

"That does not compute. You are unauthorised. Please state your purpose?" Model 306 repeated.

"Now's a good time to 'down' her. Quick, before she reports us!"

"Okay," he said, cracking his knuckles. "Someone has to do it."

He roared and charged her, wrapping his arms around her chest, expecting his momentum to knock her to the ground. It was like grabbing a brick wall. Before he knew what hit him, he was dangling upside down by one leg, shouting, "Hey! Let go!"

Model 306 opened her fist and he fell to the ground with a thud.

"Please state your purpose," she repeated with the same intonation as before.

"A word of advice, do not underestimate the females on Elemental Island." Jakob turned to the robot. "Authorisation code 300 Alpha 6." Model 306's head slumped and her eyes closed. The lights on her wrist shut down. "And that is how you immobilise a robot without any sheep-tackling experience," he added.

Danny lay on his back. "Okay, I get it. The joke is on me."

"There's nothing on you except bits of grass and some dust, and that should be quick to fix." Jakob popped open the panel on the 306's chest.

I offered my hand to Danny to help him up. He grabbed it, and sprung to his feet. "I'll tell you this much, girls here are plenty different to the ones back home." He smiled at me and I smiled back until I realised he was looking me straight in the eyes. No one else ever did that, except Grandma! Even she only did it when we were alone. I uncurled my fingers and let go of his hand. Blushing, I examined the jumble of colourful wires that snaked around in the Overseer's chest cavity, twisted, braided, and in the case of the multi-coloured ones, even fused together. The wires connected to a couple of green motherboards in the middle, with chips and tiny switches lined up in neat rows, all held in place by two large screws on the side.

Jakob frowned. "She's different from the other 300s I've seen. It's almost as if a 200 series was placed inside a 300 body."

"That's good, right?" I said. "If you can program a 300 then a 200 should be easy."

"Negative. The 200 series was manufactured before cold fusion. It uses completely different technology most of which is obsolete. I should be able to work it out, but it will take time. And a toolkit." I handed him one from my pack.

"I see you had this all planned out," he said as he opened the small satchel and laid it on the grass. Inside, there were several tiny screwdrivers, drills and tweezers. He selected a tool and undid a lower panel on the robot's chest. Once he removed it, he went into intense mode. I saw that a lot when people immersed themselves in their obsessions. The world around him had ceased to exist.

He kept muttering under his breath. "…never seen…ancient technology…power source…"

Finally, he stood straight and stretched his back. "The problem is I am not sure where the data is collected. I presume it is in the new part but I won't know unless I link the old tech with the new."

He fiddled with the wires. Suddenly, he gave a sharp cry, and fell backwards. I rushed to his side but he was already getting up.

"Wow," he said, brushing grass from his clothes. "It is inadvisable to connect 200 technology to a cold fusion power source."

"A bit shocking, was it?" Danny asked.

"Let me check your vitals," I offered, but as soon as I turned, a crackling sound came from Model 306. She jerked and the lights on her wrist blinked.

"Looks like your little friend is awake."

The robot turned to us and spoke in a deep, bellowing male voice. "Visual comparison initiated."

"Is that the 200 model speaking?"

"Must be."

From the open panel on her chest, a stream of light emerged and flickered into an image of the meadow. There were fewer cows and the trees were not as large.

"A hologram," I said, taken aback.

"A what?" Danny reached out to touch one of the cows. His hand went right through it. "A live picture? How is this possible?"

"A hologram is a physical structure that..." Jakob began, but I shushed him.

He moved closer and as the image rotated 360 degrees, he angled his head to work out the directions.

"Judging by the topography of the field, I think that *this* tree..." – he pointed to a small sapling amongst the Caribbean pine clustered at the edge of the field on the hologram – "...is the one there."

A huge calabash stood to the south of the Tiger Moth. It was at least ten metres tall, with its branches sticking out in all directions.

"That can't be right," I said. "Look, there's a house there." A bit further to the right in the hologram, there was an old-fashioned building with stairs leading up to a wide veranda.

We all peered beyond the image to the thick bush behind a small forest of Caribbean pines.

"Commencing update," Model 200 boomed. The hologram flickered to display the meadow as it was today. The house vanished behind trees and the Tiger Moth appeared.

There was a high-pitched buzz and the robot's voice cracked. "Warning! Warning! Alert Level 1. Flight equipment detected. Initiating destruction sequence. Please clear the area. Ten. Nine. Eight..."

"She's going to destroy the Scouter!" I yelled. "Do something!"

306 extended her arm towards the Tiger Moth and her wrist snapped back.

"Seven. Six..."

A nozzle protruded from the synthetic skin.

"Not on my watch, you squinty scoundrel!" Danny jumped in front of her and grabbed her hand, but she did not move.

"Please clear the area. Destruction imminent. Five. Four..."

Jakob lunged at the robot, grabbed a handful of wires and pulled. The hologram vanished. 306 slumped and smoke poured from her chest.

I shut my eyes and breathed deep.

Danny spoke first. "Thanks, brah. I think you just saved my plane."

"He saved your *life*," I said, my heart still beating fast. "If you had been standing in front of her when she got to zero, there would have been nothing left of the plane, *or* you. That was a demolition robot, wasn't it? I've seen a calcast about them. They were used years ago to help mine metals from the volcanic rock."

Jakob was white and shaking. He gave a tiny nod.

"Are you okay, brah?"

"No!' Jakob cried, starting to flap his hands. "Wiping memory is one thing, but I have no idea what the consequence is for blowing up a robot."

He was seconds away from a complete meltdown. Keeping as calm as I could, I said, "You did the right thing. The *smart* thing. Nobody was hurt. Can you reattach 306's wires without reactivating the 200 model?"

Given a clear task, he swung into motion, working fast but with precision. "Yes, I think I can." His voice was stronger. "Give me a few minutes."

I watched him use the tweezers to weave wires from the motherboard to switches and fiddle with minute screws.

"Are you trying to deactivate the old tech, so the demolition robot won't remember us?"

"Affirmative."

"Can you wipe 306's memory too?"

Jakob didn't answer for a few minutes. His concentration was total. If he ever changed his mind about his thesis on reverse electromagnetism, he could always do robotics.

Then he stood and stretched, relief written all over his face. "It's done. She won't remember us, and neither will the 200." He popped the front panel of the 306 back into place. "I've put her in slumber mode. Before we leave, I will reactivate her so no one investigates why she is not transmitting data."

"You are amazing. Even you have to admit that, Danny."

He didn't answer.

I looked up and then scanned around me in panic. "Jakob, where is Danny?"

14

I'd Rather Fight a Bio Suit than a Scavenger Any Day

"Danny," I shouted. "Danny!" A couple of cows jerked up their heads. To my surprise, tears pricked my eyes.

Danny emerged from the bushes on the other side of the field and ran back to us. "Stop yelling, sweetheart. You're scaring the cattle." He took a long look at me.

"Are you okay?" he asked. I swallowed and nodded.

"Come and see what I found!"

We jogged across the field and Danny pushed aside some prickly branches. In a nearby tree, a sloth gazed at us upside down, unafraid, with a sleepy baby clinging to her tummy. Behind them, in the middle of an overgrown garden, I saw a dilapidated building.

One of the attic windows was broken. It made the house look like it was squinting in embarrassment.

"Clear silica glass," Jakob noted. "It must have been built before they invented photosensitive coating."

I walked down a path that had grass in the cracks. Wildflowers dotted the rough garden beds. Straggly fruit trees bore custard apples and lemons and there was the scent of mint in the air. A broken swing hung by one strand from the branch of a large tree. Once this would have been a gorgeous house. I imagined it painted pale blue with white trimming and envisaged Neil and his mower let loose on the lawn. The result in my mind was much nicer than our houses back in town, which were all the same.

I walked up three steps onto the rickety veranda. Danny grabbed my hand and dragged me inside.

"Look!" he cried. "We are the first ones here for sure. I can't see any signs of scavenging. There are still light fittings and stuff all over the place!"

We had stepped into a lounge area with a faded floral couch slumped in one corner. Dull colourless curtains hung lank at the windows. I imagined them bright yellow and blue. Way prettier than my photosensitive smart window. Sunlight streamed through the silica panes, catching dust motes in the air. The floorboards creaked as we walked, but at least they seemed solid enough.

"This place is beautiful!" Danny said as he almost skipped to the next room. I followed him into what appeared to be an old Learning Hub, with hard wooden seats in rows instead of pods. All along one wall were pictures with simple instructions.

Do not touch other people!

Do not look into people's eyes!

Speak logically!

These were things Mother had said to me all my life, but I couldn't image why they would print them and hang them on a wall. Most people didn't have to learn them.

Then it hit me. This was Grandmother's retraining house! It had to be! What horrors would I find here?

"There are bedrooms down here, with beds in them!" Danny's voice was shrill with excitement. I followed him to a series of small rooms, each with a single bed, a tiny cupboard and a bed lamp on a side table. The right size for a child.

"Imagine having all this room for one person!" Danny pulled up a rat-eaten mattress and inspected the springs. "Hardly any rust at all. If we could get these back we'd make a fortune."

I imagined Grandmother as a four-year-old curled up in one of these, crying for her mother. I felt sick inside.

"I wonder if some of the first Elemental Harvesters lived here," Jakob said, standing next to me. I considered telling him about retraining houses but realised that Grandmother had shared her story in confidence. Besides, I couldn't talk about all that in front of Danny.

Just then, Danny pushed past us like an excited puppy and within moments, he called out, "This kitchen is huge!"

We followed him into a large room. The ceiling was warped and mouldy. A damp patch on the floor showed that the roof must have leaked during the last storm. Apart from a few chipped plates and cups sitting on long open shelves, I would never have guessed it was a kitchen. Where was the food printer? And the exothermer?

"What's that?" There was a large metal box that had a wide door at the front and four small round pads on top.

"You've never seen a cooker?" Danny asked.

"You cook on that? How?"

"Are you for real?" He must have guessed that I was "real," whatever that meant, so he went to the box and showed me some knobs. "You turn these, and then these" – he pointed to the discs – "heat up and you cook your food on them. Only the classiest houses have them though. The rest of us use wood burners."

"Ah," Jakob said. "Electric conduction of heat through metal. How inefficient."

"Whatever." Danny shrugged. "But this baby could set me up for years if I could get it back with me."

Right now, I didn't want to think of babies in this place.

An almighty crash shook the house. I heard a cry of pain and spun around. Jakob was gone! In his place was a gaping hole in the floor.

"Jakob!"

"Drang! That's my fault! How many times has Pa warned me to watch out for rotting floors?" Danny crouched at the edge and called down. "Are you okay, brah?"

It was pitch black. Then I heard the best sound in the world. A moan.

"He's alive!"

"Wait here." Danny ran from the kitchen.

My calpad torch lit up Jakob, sprawled on his back in what appeared to be a cellar. He rolled onto his side and coughed violently.

Danny appeared with sheets in his hands. He must have stripped them from the beds. "Quick! Help me plait them together."

He thrust the ends of three sheets into my hands. "Hold these." He started to twist the other ends together. "Never trust old material, Pa says. But if you have no rope, then plait the old stuff together. We have to get him out fast. The first few minutes can save a man's life."

Jakob started coughing again. With swift hands, Danny tied the plaited sheets around the legs of the cooker and abseiled into the abyss. I shone my torch to guide his way.

"I'm coming! Hang on."

Jakob's voice rasped. "I think you are the one hanging on."

"Good, good. Humour is a good sign." He jumped the last bit and the cellar lit up as Jakob turned on his own calpad torch.

"Don't move." Danny knelt beside Jakob and started probing his arms and legs.

"You've done this before," Jakob croaked.

"Old buildings are dangerous places. I've set many bones in my time."

"Set them where?"

As they talked, I studied the cellar. A stone staircase spiralled up one wall. It must come out there… I looked up and saw an open door. Sure enough, stairs led down and I took them two at a time.

"I'm fine!" Jakob staggered to his feet. The first thing I did was to scan him with the Medihealth option.

"Nothing broken."

"I already told him that. Lean on me, brah, and I'll help you up the stairs."

As Jakob's wrist torch flickered over the walls, ghostly figures loomed out of the dark.

"Watch out!" Danny leapt in front of us. "Those scavengers got here first! Run!"

Jakob snapped off his calpad, spread it out to its full size and light filled the room. "There are your scavengers."

"Biohaz suits," I said as my heartbeat returned to normal. Four bright yellow suits complete with respirator masks hung on racks. "What are they doing here? I haven't seen one of those since I had an immersion day at the research lab of the hospital." My mind was going into overdrive. Surely, children would not have been subjected to anything that required the use of biohaz suits. What about Grandmother…

Danny exhaled. "I'd rather fight a bio suit than a scavenger any day. Mind you, no one has had to use them since the Butterfly Kiss."

Jakob grunted. "Do you mean that people on the mainland are so afraid of butterflies that you wear biohaz suits?"

"I'm talking about the Before." Danny's voice became singsong as if he was reciting something. "Before our time, before our fathers', before our grandfathers', when our great-grandfathers were laddies."

"Is this the after-effect of flying?" Jakob asked.

"Actually," Danny said in his normal voice, "my great-grandfather wasn't even born then, but the Storyteller's was." He looked from Jakob to me. "Come on, you must know this story. About the Before. And the After. Or don't you have a Storyteller here?"

"Well, I remember Sal had a mini-obsession about drama and theatre, and she talked a *lot* about the role of the narrator..." My voice tapered off. "Is that what you mean?"

Jakob's calpad chimed. "It is 06:45. If we don't leave soon, then I will not make my SP session." It folded up and he snapped it back on his wrist.

"Sure you're okay?"

"Bit stiff and sore, but I'll be fine." He turned to Danny. "Thank you for your help and concern. It was...unexpected."

"Any time, brah."

We headed up the steps and Danny asked, "If you are going back to town now, what will I do?"

Jakob and I exchanged a glance. We hadn't thought that far. In the kitchen, we all walked a wide path around the hole.

"I could stay here for a while." He gestured to the house. "Maybe you could stay with me? Rest a bit," he said to Jakob. "You could tell me more about hope machines and stuff. Astie could go see about the fuel."

There was that tone again. I didn't understand Danny. One moment he's about to save us from strangers in the dark and the next I didn't trust him at all. I knew that under no circumstances should I leave the two of them alone, despite how friendly they were becoming. I opened my mouth to object, but Jakob beat me to it.

"That is not possible." He sounded almost shocked. "It is not in my calpad." He pushed it under Danny's nose. "I have scheduled activities that must be adhered to. See? 09:30–10:30 Relaxation session at the Sensory Park. 11:00 Evening meal. 12:30 Space Seekers begins." He got louder as he read each entry.

"What do you mean? Don't you ever do anything without planning it first?"

"No. That would be illogical."

"I prefer to call it an adventure," Danny replied, and I secretly agreed. I longed for days that were not structured to the minute. This day had been close to ideal.

"Okay, then *I'll* come with *you*," Danny announced. "Let me go grab some stuff from the Scouter." Without waiting for an answer, he ran out of the kitchen. We heard the door open and his feet pounding down the veranda steps.

"So can he come with us?" I asked Jakob. "It will only be until I find the fuel."

He didn't answer and as we left the house, I let him think on it. Walking down the cracked path, I glanced back and tried to imagine it as Grandmother would have seen it sixty years ago. A crisp lawn, pretty gardens, a wide veranda to catch the breeze. Maybe the sloth's grandmother watched mine play on the swing. Perhaps the worst thing was to be apart from her family. I hoped I was right. One day, I would make Grandmother tell me the truth. When I was ready to hear it. We forced our way through the dense vegetation and the house disappeared from sight again, with its secrets intact.

15

Monitors Are Coming!

Danny was already at the Tiger Moth, standing on a wing, as the two of us walked back to 306. Jakob started the process of reactivating her. He began to relax as he worked on something he understood.

"Astie, I have been thinking."

I gulped. I was not sure I wanted to hear what he had to say.

"It is impossible for you to obtain enough gasoline. For a start, even if you could locate it, you would have no means of transporting it."

I kept quiet. After all, what could I say?

"If indeed, Danny is stranded here, then we cannot hide him for ever," he continued. "We have achieved our initial goal of observing a flight machine. I have wiped the Overseer's memory for you and we will not be discovered. There are only so many rules I am prepared to break and I've reached my limit. We have to report him as soon as we get back."

"You're joking, right?"

"He's a stranger from the mainland, Astie. He's a risk to the community."

"He *risked* his life for you! He jumped down that hole to save you and then was prepared to fight off scavengers while you ran to safety."

"I like Danny and he proved himself to be brave, but my feelings and his actions do not negate a law."

"I can't believe this. I know rules are rules, but some rules just don't make sense. Have you thought about what the Monitors would do to him? We can hide him until we think of a way of getting him off the island."

I forced myself to stop talking. Arguing facts with Jakob was futile. He always won that game. I had to give him time to think things through. He kept working on the robot in silence.

I thought things through too. What *would* they do to Danny if they caught him? Would they take him away, as they had done with Grandmother? Not to the same house, obviously, but still... He was the first interesting thing that had come into my life, ever! I ached to help him somehow. Jakob *had* to change his mind!

There was a crack of a breaking twig and I turned around. Danny was right behind us. Had he heard our conversation? I looked at him and my jaw dropped. Jakob followed my glance and asked the obvious question. "Why are you wearing those?"

Danny took off a pair of dark glasses and held them up. "What's wrong with sunglasses?"

"Nobody wears glasses here."

"Not at all? What if you can't see well? My Grandpops is blind as a bat without his."

"Bats use echolocation, not sight," Jakob said.

"Why doesn't your Grandpops get his eyes fixed?" I asked. "Jakob was born blind and the nanobots healed him before he was a day old."

"For real?" Danny came closer and peered into Jakob's eyes. I stepped between them. We didn't have time for a fight.

"Yes, *for real*," I agreed. "Besides, we all have nano-coating on our eyes against UV rays so no need for sunglasses. Better take those off or anyone who sees you will know you do not belong here."

Danny popped the glasses into his backpack.

Jakob closed the front panel of 306. If he thought that Danny had heard us, he wasn't letting on either. "Let's go," he said. "I've put the Overseer into slumber mode. That gives us five minutes to get out of her sight before she regains all her functions."

He handed me the toolkit and the three of us headed for the edge of the meadow and the relative protection of the trees there. I took a last longing look at the Tiger Moth. One day, I promised myself, I was going to fly.

Once we were behind the tree line, Danny fell in step with Jakob. I was glad to let them talk together. The terrible thought of betraying my new friend gnawed at me, but I knew that Jakob would not understand my feelings at all. No one on the island ever felt guilty about following rules. That would be illogical.

"So tell me more about this hope machine you are designing," I heard Danny ask Jakob. "Maybe I could help you. Pa taught me to maintain the Scouter, so I know quite a bit about how she's built."

Jakob hesitated. Ah, I thought to myself. *Now* it occurs to him that he's talking to someone he's planning to betray. Someone who had just rescued him.

"Perhaps," he said at last. "Can you explain how the braking system works?"

I tuned out of their conversation and marched ahead. The sun was hot and before long, I was wishing Danny would offer to take my pack again. I wouldn't turn him down this time. The climbing was hard and the rocks were scorching under my hands.

"Hey," Danny called up to me. "Isn't that one of those pineapple things?"

I saw a Skywater vessel silhouetted on the top of the ridge and angled my route towards it. The boys caught up to me and we reached it together. I took my bottle from my pack, filled it and drank. Jakob did the same. I watched intrigued as Danny leaned down and drank straight from the tap, with water dribbling down his chin. He then refilled his flask.

"Perhaps while we are here," Jakob suggested, "you can take the opportunity to wash your face and hands before we head into town. This will not improve your body odour of course, but will make you more presentable."

"Thanks, brah! You smell like a rose yourself."

"He's sort of right, though, Danny. No one over the age of five gets as dirty as you are."

In a huff, Danny splashed water over his face and wiped himself dry with his shirt-sleeve.

"Happy now?"

"Better."

"Why are your shoes wet?" Jakob asked.

"Um, I got water on them."

"All our clothes are hydrophobic," I explained. "They never get wet."

"Your shirt is dry," Jakob pointed out.

Danny touched his chest. "Brill," he said. "I could sure use more of these back home."

I tapped my calpad. "Let's get moving. We have a long way to go."

I turned around to start the descent, and then ducked, flattening myself to the rocks and soil. "Stay down," I hissed. "Monitors!" The boys dropped to the ground beside me.

Three white dune buggies with a large M painted in red on the side were speeding along the beach road, leaving a cloud of dust behind them.

"They could be heading for the meadows!" My heart was beating in my throat.

"Do you think it's me they're after?" Danny asked.

"Could 306 have reported anything, Jakob?"

"I'm almost certain I wiped all the relevant bits from her hard disk." He sounded less than sure.

"Maybe you're not as good as you imagine you are," Danny said quietly.

"I am good, but the manipulation required to erase memory from both a 200 and 300 series is problematic. It is possible that while her old tech was connected, she registered the flight machine as a threat. Some of that could have remained in her RAM."

Danny huffed. "It was too hard for you and you botched it. Now the sheriffs are after us. Perfect!"

"That would not be perfect at all," I disagreed. "It could mean that they are looking for your plane. They would have to follow the beach road past the hills and then take the service road to the meadow, but they would be there in little more than an hour."

"And once they see it, it won't take a genius to realise that the Scouter needs a pilot." He rubbed his chin. "Well, as Pa says, trouble *is* my middle name."

It was such an odd thing to say that I ignored it. Instead, I asked Jakob, "What are we going to do?"

He got to his feet and scampered behind the water tower where he would not be spotted, and started flapping his hands. "I don't know! I should never have listened to you, Astatine!"

Danny raised his eyebrows. "Astatine?" he repeated. "Cute."

I crawled low until I too could stand safely. "Think, Jakob!" I kept my voice low and calm. If he went into a meltdown now we would be caught for certain. "Is there any way that the Monitors will be able to tell that the Overseer was tampered with?"

"Yes," he nodded frantically. "When I took the screws from the front panel, there would have been dust scraped away at least, maybe some minute scratches, and a Monitor would tell right away that some wires were cut inside."

"Okay." I stayed as calm as I could. This was not good. Not good at all.

"I don't think it will be the robot they'd be interested in. At least not at first," Danny said.

He was still lying on his stomach watching the vehicles below. I studied the meadow. I couldn't see the Tiger Moth from this angle, but if that's where the Monitors were heading, they were sure to find it.

"Besides, if they do catch me, I could always say *I* opened her up," Danny offered.

"You?" I was stunned.

"Why not? I could pretend that robots were my 'thesis' and I was curious."

"That is a falsehood!" Jakob's flapping stopped.

"It's a 'falsehood' that will save your butt." Danny got to his feet and stood beside us.

"You would lie for us?"

"I just said I would, didn't I? That's what friends do. *Protect* each other. *Not inform* Monitors about things they don't need to know." He looked at me in that peculiar way and I knew that he had heard us talking about reporting him. I was impressed. Instead of confronting us with facts, he had worked on our emotions. It was such a clever technique that it might even be successful on Jakob. I gave Danny the barest nod, and he nodded back. We were on the same side, wherever that would lead.

"Jakob," I said, "do you agree that the Code Red rule applies to strangers only?"

He chewed his lips for a moment and replied, "That's correct."

"But Danny is not a stranger. We know his name. We've spent a whole day with him. Plus, he's our *friend* because he put himself in danger to help us *and* he is prepared to protect us if he gets caught."

"That's irrelevant," Jakob replied, but I heard hesitation in his voice. I pressed on.

"Well, do you at least agree that the main purpose of Code Red is to eliminate the danger of contagion?" Mother would be proud of my logic.

He thought about it. "Yes, but..."

"We have both seen that he is not contagious, right, so no need to report that?" I interrupted.

"Perhaps..."

"And..." I breathed deep. Everything hinged on the next bit. "...do you agree that there is no rule to report a friend even if Monitors should find his flight machine?"

Jakob stood frozen. His mind had to be in overdrive. To help him along, I repeated, almost in a whisper, "No stranger, no contagion and no threat. No need to report a thing. Danny can stay out of sight for a few days and you go back to your thesis."

Both Danny and I held our breath.

16

Cloud Surfing on the Run

It's amazing how long fifteen seconds can feel when you are not breathing. I willed Jakob to see it my way and not report Danny.

Finally, he said, "Where will he go?"

I breathed out in relief. We'd won! "Maybe my house for now?" I suggested. "He could hide in the cat runs. No one would look for him there."

"What's a cat run?" Danny asked, screwing up his face, but I shushed him.

"Jakob? Is that okay?"

He glanced at me. "Just for tonight, Astie. Then we will see if we can find the fuel so he can leave Elemental Island and go back to wherever he came from. Agreed?"

"Thanks, brah," Danny said, and went to slap him on the back, then stopped himself.

Jakob checked his calpad. "We better get going. My session starts in fifty-two minutes."

We were panting and sweaty when we reached the edge of town. Jakob ran ahead so he'd be on time. Danny's eyes flickered at every movement when we reached the paved streets.

"This place is unnatural. Everything's so clean and neat. Back home there's rubbish and graffiti everywhere."

"What's graffiti?"

"You know, drawing stuff on walls and things."

"Without permission?"

"It's not something you ask permission for."

"But that's against the rules."

"People do lots of things against the rules where I come from, sweetheart."

"Like what?"

Danny didn't answer at first, then said, "When you and your family are hungry or sick or in danger, what is right and what is wrong start to blur. The rules aren't so clear no more."

"Well, rules are sure clear here."

"So I've seen. Where's your house?"

"About fifteen minutes away."

"Do we have to walk through town? Can we take a back route?"

"Whichever way we go, there will be people around."

Danny grabbed my arm. "Like them," he nodded towards the intersection. I bit back a gasp.

"Monitors! Whatever you do, don't take off your cap or show that gap in your teeth."

He pulled the brim down so it shielded most of his face. "What are we going to do?!"

"Keep going. To run will get their attention."

Danny stiffened as he walked. All ease had gone from his swagger. Perfect. He fitted in better that way. The two Monitors ignored us as they spoke in serious tones to each other.

"Look ahead of you at a forty-five degree angle. Don't ever look anyone in the eye," I whispered as a woman glided by on free-wheeler bike that propelled itself. This was harder than expected. "And make sure you don't bump into anyone or brush past them." I shook my head slightly. "You made me sound just like Mother." She had been saying these sorts of things to me since I was a toddler. *Now* I understood how important it was for her that I fit in.

A dog barked behind its invisible fence and Danny flinched. "At least you have a mother. Mine died when I was born."

I was speechless. No woman ever died in childbirth on the island. Danny's people did not have the med droids that we had, and he knew nothing of nanobots. I was starting to get a picture of his life on the mainland and it was not a pretty one.

"I'm sorry," I whispered.

"Yeah, me too."

A low "reep, reep" sound behind us made us turn. It was the siren of a Monitor vehicle. Other cars cleared the road and it zoomed past at speed, its sleek black surface hiding its occupants. Another one was racing towards us.

"This way!" I scooted into a side street. "They must be looking for you, for sure. I've never seen so many Monitors in one day."

Danny ducked behind a tree, then flattened himself to the ground and crept along on his elbows in the shadow of a bush.

"What on earth are you doing?"

"Making sure I'm not seen. Pa and I always do this when we scout a new place."

"Well it won't work here. If you are seen doing that, everyone will know you do not belong. Get up."

But Danny lay there gawking at the bush. "It's got apples and oranges and plums all growing on the same branch!"

"Clever, isn't it?" I agreed. "Many people choose grafting as a special interest for a while. But now's not the time to admire the vegetation."

Danny got up and brushed the leaves off his shirt. Just in time!

Two Monitors marched towards us, but it was clear their minds were not on two minors.

"Yeah, the meadows," one said as they passed. "Code Red One."

"I've got children!" the other replied. "I'll do anything to keep them safe!"

"We've got to get off the streets," I hissed. "This way!" I scampered around the corner and saw the cluster of people waiting at the gates to the Sensory Park. It must be change-over time. The previous group was filing out the exit at the far end. Jakob was one of the first people in when the entrance gates opened. He headed straight for the stretch-and-squeeze hammock. Once he curled up in there I knew he would not emerge until the session ended. He had a lot of tension to be stretched and squeezed out.

"I have an idea. Follow me. Act casual." We mingled with the crowd entering through the gates. "I'm sure no Monitor would think to look here for a flight machine fugitive."

"What is this place?" Danny asked, breaking my rules and staring like a child.

"It's the Sensory Park. Don't you have one?"

"Nope."

I tried to see it through his eyes. All the contraptions and devices *would* be confusing to someone who has never seen them before.

We strode past a tall, clear, cylindrical tower.

"What's that?"

"It's a wind tunnel. It shoots up high-pressure air and you float on it. It's like flying, but without danger, because you don't go that high."

"What? Like a bird?"

"Yeah. It's the only kind of flight allowed. Now, without being obvious, check for something that no one is on. You have to book ahead for the device you want and we don't want to argue with anyone about whose turn it is."

We passed people squeezing through roller mats and twirling on swings. One girl sat mesmerized in front of a display of bright lights as she fiddled with strands of beads that vibrated in her hands. "That one's better at night," I explained.

There was another "reep, reep" in the distance and Danny grabbed my hand and tugged me towards the squish tunnels, a series of pipes where you could loop the loop and slide to your heart's content.

I pulled my hand away. "No, someone's already on it."

"But there's heaps of room for three people."

"People don't like to be crowded or touched. We always have uninterrupted time on an activity by ourselves. Over there – the Sky Surfer is free. That one can be booked as a paired activity."

I jogged towards four posts that towered into the sky and stood in the centre on a large X. Danny came beside me and shrugged. "Now what?"

I waved to Albert, the Park Keeper, who was watching us from his booth. I knew him well. He was a Level One and loved nothing more than operating the equipment around him.

We floated into the air. Danny fell onto his back as we rose higher and higher on an invisible carpet.

"What's happening!" he squeaked.

"Shut your eyes and feel the material under you," I commanded. Now was *not* the time for a meltdown. "If you freak out, people will notice you." I watched as he obeyed, then he opened one eye and shut it immediately.

"I can feel something there, but I can't see it."

"It's an elemental polypropylene mat. It's 2D so it looks transparent. You can't be afraid of heights, otherwise how would you fly your plane? We should be able to see what the Monitors are doing."

Danny sat up and looked around with eyes the size of saucers. We were rising at a steady pace. From here, we could see the beach and the jagged curved ridge that led to the meadows.

"There's my house," I said as it came into view.

"Rad."

"Now, be careful you don't fall off." I started running and jumped into the air…

Danny yelped, "No!!!!"

…and I ricocheted off an invisible wall, somersaulted and landed with a bounce.

"We're in a box." I grinned at the expression on his face. "You can sit there if you're scared. I understand. You're only a boy."

That remark made Danny get to his feet so fast he wobbled a bit on the spongy surface. He was beaming.

"This," he said, "must be the craziest thing I've ever done in my life!"

He got used to cloud surfing in no time at all, and soon we were somersaulting and flipping high above the island. Then I caught a glimpse of a dust cloud on the Beach Road and lay on my stomach squinting into the distance.

"There are five, six, no... seven cars heading towards the meadow. They've definitely found your plane."

"And your town is swarming with Monitors. There's a group there, and over there, and one by that place… Is it full of bubbles?"

"Yeah, Rainbow Square. I see them. As soon as this session ends, we need to get back to my place. You'll be safe there." I finger-wrote a route into the air. "If we go down *that* street and cut through *that* alley we should dodge all the Monitors. And don't forget, most likely they will be searching for an adult, not a 'goat' like you."

"You mean a kid?"

"I might do."

A gentle chime filled the air and our invisible box began to lower. "Time's up. Most people will have a second session scheduled, but we should slip out before Jakob sees us. He won't approve of us sneaking in without an appointment."

"That was unreal." We both stumbled a little on the solid ground. "Pa will never believe I did that."

By the time Jakob emerged from his squeezy cocoon, we were long gone. Once we reached the alley, we saw no more Monitors and I relaxed a little. We were going to make it yet.

"You know," I said as we turned into my street, "I have done more unscheduled things today than in my entire life."

"Was it fun?" Danny bumped into my arm roughly and I stepped back.

"Why did you do that?" I asked.

"Drang, I'm sorry. You people really have something against body contact, don't you? Where I come from, this is how we say we like each other. How do *you* tell someone you like them and enjoy being with them?"

I thought of Grandmother's hugs, but I could never tell him that. "I say, thanks for a great day. I enjoyed it very much."

"I guess that would be clear."

"We like clear here."

We walked a little further in silence and then without warning I leaned over and bumped against his arm.

Danny grinned. He bumped me back and said, "Thanks for a great day. I enjoyed it very much."

17

Stand By for an Unscheduled Calcast

"Hey." I came to a sudden halt. "Look at that!"

Blue Tail was crossing the street sauntering towards us.

"Crazy cat's stalking us," Danny said, but he allowed the cat to curl around his legs. "I wonder how she got that paint on her tail."

"No idea," I said innocently, "but maybe if we take her home, I can clean her up a bit."

Danny picked her up and she purred contentedly in his arms. As we turned the corner into my street, my calpad read 10:27. I checked the bicycle stand, but the only bike there was mine. "They're not home yet, but let me make sure. Wait here."

The door slid open for me. "I'm back," I said in a voice loud enough to provoke an immediate shushing from Mother. Dad's cats came meowing to greet me, but other than that, there was no response. I turned around and motioned for Danny to come in.

He stood at the entrance, his mouth open wide, hugging Blue Tail to him as the other cats meowed up at her. "What's all that?" he asked, staring at Father's cat runs, spiral stairs and cat-shaped holes in the wall.

"Dad likes cats."

"Me too." Danny followed me to the kitchen trying not to trip over Black Cat. "But mostly because they catch rats."

"Would you like a drink of water?" I asked. My Medihealth function had been vibrating a while now, reminding me to rehydrate. I reached into the cupboard for a glass, then waved my hand in front of a glowing blue button by the sink. Danny's jaw dropped as water poured from the tap.

"You wave and there's water?" he asked.

"Cold and hot." I showed him the blue and red lights.

"Skrate! That's amazing. Grandpops built a pump in our kitchen, but most people use the well."

Now that was a crazy thought. Why would you have a well in your kitchen? I didn't want to insult his home, so I didn't comment. Instead, I tapped the food printer and two chicken pies appeared. I touched them. Too cold. That printer never got it quite right.

I placed the pies in the exothermer to heat them, ignoring Danny's open mouth. I couldn't very well keep explaining every kitchen appliance. I took Blue Tail from him, handed him the steaming hot food on a plate, and ushered him down the hall with a couple of the cats following us.

As we reached my room, the door slid open. Danny, who had already bitten into the pie, jumped backwards and made choking noises. "The door opened all by itself," he croaked.

"Yes," I nodded. "How do your doors open?"

"With a handle."

"You mean that everyone uses the same handle?"

"Well, we don't carry around separate ones."

"Eww," I said, screwing up my face. "Think of all the germs!"

The door shut behind us. I put Blue Tail down on my bed where she sniffed around then curled up on my pillow as if she owned the place. I waved my fingers in the air and my favourite music began to play. Danny froze. Maybe he has sound sensitivities, I thought, so I waved my fingers again and the music stopped. I flicked the air, the shutters drew apart and my windows opened. Danny stood like a Zombie from Space Seekers.

"It's just a girl's bedroom," I laughed. "Nothing to be afraid of."

"How did this..." he flicked his fingers, "...do that?" He pointed to the window.

"The movements are connected to the wall calpad of course."

"Of course," he echoed, and then gazed around the room.

"It's huge. A whole family could sleep in here!"

I hurried to pick up the clothes from the floor and threw them into the washing chute. Danny didn't seem to mind the mess though.

"You have a rad room, but why are all your houses the same from the outside?" he asked.

"Why should they be different? Most families are the same size, with two children. The families that have a permit for three are housed in a different cluster."

"Wow, you have to have a permit to have kids?"

He wandered around touching this and that and stopped in front of my designs covering the walls. "What's all that? You like to draw?"

"I like clothes." I braced myself for his look of disgust, but Danny nodded. He took a large bite of the second pie and chewed fast.

"This is delicious."

"Mother will have the evening meal ready for us soon. I'll try to sneak you some more food afterwards."

"You get more food than this to eat? Skrate!" He slumped down on my bed and stroked Blue Tail. I sat in my pod.

"Doesn't anyone work around here?" he asked. "Do you?"

"I'm still studying."

"Everyone is walking on the streets doing nothing. And there were grown-ups at the park where we left Jakob. How come they have time to play?"

"Today and tomorrow are rest days. Don't you have rest days on the mainland?"

"People rest when they are tired, I suppose. There is no special day for it. Kids can play when they have finished their chores. You start training though when you are seven, and after that there isn't much time for it."

"Training for what?"

"Whatever your pa does. I'm lucky my pa is the Scout. Nothing beats it. We get to be adventurers. I think it's even better than being the Storyteller, though everybody makes such a big deal of that."

"Why? What's a storyteller, then?"

"Most towns have one. You can go and ask him if you scavenge something that you don't know how to use. He knows about the Before. And once a month, the adults go to the Storytelling Hut to listen to him speak."

"What about children? Aren't they allowed?"

"Yeah, when you turn thirteen. The first time you go, he tells you a story that's yours alone. He shares a piece of the Before with you to show that you are now a full member of the community."

"So, you've done that already?" I wondered what story he'd been told.

He nodded. "And I've been going to the Storytelling Hut ever since with Pa."

"What is this Before? And how does the Storyteller know about it?"

"From Father to Son to Son to Son," he said in a singsong voice. He took another bite of the pie and added in his normal voice, "They've been doing it for generations."

"What if you want to be a storyteller but your father does something different?"

He shrugged. "I guess you're out of luck then. You *could* train for something other than what your pa does, I suppose, but I wouldn't know how to go about it."

I thought for a second. "What about girls?" I asked.

Danny swallowed the last bite of pie. "Most girls don't train. They cook, clean, work the land, tend to the animals and have babies. Kinda boring, if you ask me."

"You can thank this boring girl for saving you from the Monitors." I turned away from him.

"Hey." He put a hand on my shoulder, turning me back. I was about to shake off his hand when he added, "You are not like other girls, Astie."

"So people keep saying. But tell me about this Before?"

He opened his mouth to answer, when I heard the murmur of voices down the hall.

"Shhh," I mouthed to him. "They're home. I'll be right back."

"What if someone comes in?" he whispered.

The idea was bizarre. "Why would they do that?"

"Where I live, people come into each other's rooms all the time without knocking."

I shook my head. "Don't worry. No one does that here. Keep quiet though." With that, I stepped into the corridor and the door slid closed behind me.

In the kitchen, Mother was programming the food printer. Father and Jon were setting the table.

"There," she said. "We eat in five minutes. Did you have a productive day at the beach, Astatine?"

"Thank you, Mother, I did." If she knew just how productive!

The front door chimed. "Who could that be, at this time of the day?" Father tapped the family calpad and Grandmother's face filled the screen. "It's

Hannah. Four minutes before the evening meal," he said to Mother. He didn't raise his voice but I could tell he was annoyed. The front door opened and Grandmother appeared in the kitchen with a cheery wave.

"Hello everyone! Hi Muffin." She winked at me behind Mother's back. "I've bought you something, like I promised."

She held up an old box. I had forgotten all about her idea for my thesis. Last night seemed a lifetime ago.

"Great!" I said as brightly as I could while my mind went into overdrive. I had to stop her from coming into my room.

"What's that?" Jon poked the package, but Grandmother pulled it away. "It's for Astie's thesis. You'll find out in due time but for now, keep your dirty paws off it."

"I don't have paws, and if I did, they would not be dirty."

Mother cut into the banter. "Would you like to stay for a meal with us?"

Grandmother shook her head. "No, I ate already." She sat down in Jon's chair. "I'll have a tea in the meantime." Mother's face showed no reaction, but I knew that comment would irk her. Grandmother never stuck to a schedule. She did things when it pleased her. I think my family would choke if they had to eat before 11:00.

I stifled a smile as Jon's shoulders slumped when Mother asked him to bring in another chair. Grandmother remained in Jon's seat knowing his manners would not allow him to complain. I know she loves him, but he was so easy to tease.

Mother put the food on the table at exactly 11:00. We had each taken our portion when the family calpad switched itself on and the image of the announcer filled the kitchen wall. Father glanced up from his plate of chicken wings. "This is the most unusual evening meal, full of interruptions," he sighed. "What is going on now?"

It was my favourite announcer, a blonde woman, who always sounded cheerful. Now her voice quivered.

"Stand by for an unscheduled calcast."

18

What Do You Know About the Off-Landers?

Mother frowned. "I don't recall ever having an unscheduled calcast before." She was focusing hard on the calpad as if that would make the intruder disappear.

Councillor Lena appeared on the screen with a group of men and women behind her. Everyone looked sombre. Her aide, a middle-aged man, was biting his lips and chewing the ends of his moustache.

Father waved at the calpad to initiate the 3D option and a hologram of Lena appeared in our kitchen, her hair pulled back in a neat white bun. I looked at the freckles on her face, clearly visible in 3D, and remembered Grandmother once telling me that in her youth Lena's hair had been ginger.

"Citizens, neighbours and friends," she said. "It has been my privilege to lead you for the past fourteen years. My philosophy has always been one of complete openness. Even though what I am about to tell you might come as a shock to you all, I have no right to withhold the truth from you." She hesitated for a moment. I had a sinking feeling in the pit of my stomach that I knew exactly what she was about to say.

"For generations, we have led quiet lives on Elemental Island, with little or no interruption to our cherished routines. Now, something has happened to disrupt that, although I trust that we as a community are strong enough to handle it." She took a deep breath. "This afternoon at 09:23 an object was discovered in the far meadow. At first, all we could ascertain was that it is of foreign origin."

"What does that mean?" Jon asked, but Mother shushed him.

"After a brief examination, our Council of Science has concluded that the object is a flight machine. Although the technology it uses is crude and outdated, the fact that it has landed here proves that it is capable of flight." An image of the Tiger Moth surrounded by Monitors appeared in our kitchen.

"At last," I heard Grandmother mutter under her breath, so quietly that I would never have caught it, had I not been sitting right beside her. The others kept their eyes on the hologram and didn't seem to have noticed. Had I imagined it?

There was a close-up of the two seats. "As you can see, the machine has space for a driver and a passenger."

They knew about Danny! My legs shook under the table. I felt Grandmother watching me. When I turned to her, she looked me straight in the eyes and her face had an odd expression. "Members of the Medical Council presume that any humans travelling in it will have been killed in flight. However, no human or other remains have been found at the site." Councillor Lena was back on the screen, with a frown on her face. "The off-landers may have developed protective gear to keep them intact in the air. They could be among us."

Lena looked straight at us. "Please remain calm. There is no cause for panic. The Elemental Harvesters left us a protocol for this scenario. Rest assured that this protocol is being followed to the letter. Code Red One has been activated. I repeat. Code Red One has been activated. If anyone has information about the off-landers, please contact the Monitors. If you have seen anything else out of the ordinary, please report it to the authorities without delay."

Code Red One again. What would Jakob make of this?

"The Council of Monitors is organising a search party from first light. Volunteers can join the search by reporting to Central Hall throughout the day. Citizens, friends, neighbours! United we are strong. I am counting on your help to safeguard Elemental Island."

The calpad crackled and turned itself off. Jon broke the silence.

"The off-landers must be dead," he said. "No one can survive flight, especially open to the elements. Most likely, they exploded over the oceans somewhere and the machine drifted here on air currents. I bet their entrails are splattered everywhere."

"Jon, don't say such terrible things!" Grandmother's voice was stern.

"That *is* a conceivable scenario, Jon," Father conceded, "however, we must do as Councillor Lena asks and be on the watch for strangers. Astatine, did you see anything out of the ordinary at the beach?"

I held on to the image of children playing in the sand. I learned long ago that not telling the whole truth got me out of a lot of trouble. "No," I answered.

"So, you were at the beach today, were you, Astie?" Grandmother asked, eyeing the hiking boots I was wearing.

I nodded. Strictly speaking, this was correct since we had set off from there, but I thought it better not to say too much. If anyone could see through my lies, it would be Grandmother.

"Tomorrow morning," Father said, "I will render my services to the Monitors to seek this stranger."

"I will come with you." Mother looked at Jon.

"I can't," Jon whined. "I have SP at 02:00. I managed to book the wind tunnel." We all knew how much he liked that. It wasn't worth his tantrum to try to stop him. He surprised us all by adding "I can help after that though. I was scheduled to work on my thesis, but I can delay it for an issue as important to our security as this."

Father accessed the calpad schedule and changed his and mother's slots for the next day to read "02:00 Search team." Jon had already entered SP at 02:00 and now added "03:00 Search team."

"What about you, Astatine?" Mother prompted. "Your schedule appears to be empty."

"Um, I was planning on staying in all morning to work on my fashion designs."

A frown flickered across Mother's forehead, but before she could say anything Grandmother sighed. She put her hands over her face and leaned her arms on the table. "I'm too old to be of much use, I'm afraid, and this is such a shock for me." She *seemed* devastated, but somehow I didn't believe it. Mother took the jug of lemon mint tea, refilled Grandmother's glass and placed it beside her. It was one of Mother's ways I loved. If she saw someone upset, she'd always do something nice for that person.

"Astatine," Father chastised, as he typed SI for special interest into my slot, "you must try harder to update the home calpad. One day we will need to contact you and will have no idea where you are."

"I guess there will be enough volunteers without the two of you," Mother added.

Grandmother sat up straight and took a sip from her drink. "Thank you, Daisy Sue," she said. "I can't believe I have lived to see Code Red One activated!"

We turned to our food. I ate fast, crunching the chicken wings under my teeth, paying little attention to the talk around the table. Jon gulped down a tan-coloured blob of molecular gel and I shuddered. Jello with chicken flavour was not my idea of a good meal. He continued to ask Father never-ending questions about the technical specifications of the flight machine. Hah! I thought to myself. For once "Zero Six" knows more than her whole family put together. Pity I couldn't wow them with my brilliance. When I finished, Grandmother stood and gathered up the box.

"Let's go to your room, Astie."

I kept my face calm. "I'll take it!" I said, and went to lift it out of her hands, but she pulled away. "No. I want to talk to you about what is inside," she insisted and headed down the hall. I ran after her, talking as loudly as I dared. I hoped I would be noisy enough for Danny to hear, but not so disturbing that Mother would comment.

"It's so nice to have you over, Grandmother. You should come visit more often and not just because of my thesis. How long has it been since you've been in my room?" By the time I uttered the last sentence, we were at my door. It slid open. There was no sign of Danny.

I unclenched my jaw. Grandmother sat down on the bed beside Blue Tail who was sleeping. I was sure I heard a faint "Oomph," and coughed to cover the sound as I imagined the bottom of the mattress bumping Danny's body.

She patted the cat. "Is this one new? What has your father done to its tail? Some sort of pigment experiment?"

"Kind of," I said.

Grandmother opened the box and despite the fear of Danny's discovery, I leaned in closer to look.

"What is it?"

Grandmother lifted out a space suit similar to the ones the characters wore on Space Seekers.

"Ah," I said, "it's beautiful."

"I know this is not quite the right time to talk about fashion," she admitted, "but your thesis has to be submitted very soon."

"It's amazing!" I fingered the soft silver fabric. It was similar to a biohaz suit, but thick red arches overhung the shoulder pads, diving to a V shape at the centre of the chest. The sleeves were encrusted with beads that sparkled like diamonds, and the high neck was clasped shut with a row of dark stone buttons. A long thin rocket ship was emblazed along one arm.

"When I came up with the concept for the digicast," Grandmother said, "I designed this costume for it."

"You thought up Space Seekers? How come you never told me? You can't stand it now."

"Well, I wrote the first episode, *The Adventurers*. But it didn't go in the direction I hoped it would and I didn't want to be associated with it."

"The costumes sure didn't. This is way nicer than the one they use now."

"The programmers thought it looked too uncomfortable so they deleted all the frills in the digitalisation process."

"Why didn't *you* do fashion as your thesis? You would have been amazing at it."

Grandmother shrugged. "It wasn't an option back then. This costume is the single piece of clothing I have ever designed, but you can do so much more, Astie. Put the Space Seekers logo on shirts and caps and shoes and your thesis may well be the most popular ever."

I thought of Danny and the jacket he wore. And the scarf. I already had more ideas than Grandmother knew about.

"Do you think I could? Would it be accepted?"

"Well, it's not illegal or dangerous, but it will be up to you though to present it in such a way that *you* will be accepted along with your idea."

Grandmother draped the costume across the bed and turned to me.

"Astie, what do you think about this flight machine?" She patted Blue Tail who purred under her touch.

"It's ah, all a bit scary."

"That's for sure," Grandmother agreed. "This place won't know what hit it. All these years of never thinking beyond Elemental Island, and now the 'beyond' has come to us. I wonder where the poor driver and the passenger are. They must be terrified."

"Grandmother," I hesitated, "when we watched the news in the kitchen, I thought I heard you say, '*At last.*' What did you mean by that?"

Grandmother smiled. "Ah Muffin, you are too bright for your own good. I could lie to you and make up a reason, but we know each other too well for lies."

I swallowed as I thought of the "lie" she was sitting on.

"Let's just say that I have long had reasons for believing there is much more 'out' there and now I *know* there is. Do you understand that life is never going to be the same again?"

I knew that *my* life would never be the same. Even if Jakob and I got Danny off the island, I would never forget him. If he was caught…well, I did not want to think about that at all.

Grandmother tilted her head to the side. "So when are you going to tell me what you know about the off-landers?"

19

We've All Done Things We Regret

"What…what makes you think I know anything?" I gulped.

"Call it a hunch. Much like me, I don't think you were shocked when they showed the image of that flight machine, but you were nervous when they mentioned the driver and passenger." She gestured to my feet. "And I know your dress sense is different, but even you wouldn't wear hiking boots to the beach."

At that moment, there was a stifled sneeze. I put my hand on my nose and mumbled, "Excuse me," but Grandmother was not fooled. She jumped to her feet. "Astie, you didn't!" she said. "You can't have." She scrambled backwards, away from the bed. "You brought them here!?"

Before I could say anything, Danny crawled out with his hands in the air.

"Sorry miss. Sorry Ma'am," he said, his voice shaking. "I was running from the sheriffs and the window was open. I snuck in and hid under that there bed. I meant no harm."

Why was he saying that? Then I caught on. He was lying to protect me. Grandmother's eyes narrowed.

"And I guess you found my grandson's clothes under the bed too?" she said, recognising the shirt she had given Jon.

"Ah, no Ma'am. I found them in…another room."

Grandmother sank onto my pod, never taking her eyes off Danny. Now *she* was shaking. "Astie, what have you done!?" She held up her calpad to Danny.

"He's not contagious," I managed to say and showed her my own screen. As she studied it, her shoulders lowered and her breathing steadied. Then she gave a little laugh. "Why am I not surprised? If anyone was going to hide an off-lander it was going to be you, Muffin."

Danny snorted at the endearment, but quickly reverted to looking pathetic and harmless.

"What is your name?" Grandmother asked him.

"Danny." He did not look at her when he spoke. This boy learnt fast.

"Where is the other off-lander?"

"There's no one else, Ma'am. I came alone."

"It's true Grandmother. No one else is with him."

"Can you tell me one good reason why I should not report you immediately?"

Without missing a beat, Danny answered, "Ah, you are kind and generous, and a good woman, and you don't want a poor boy like me to get into trouble."

"Huh, that twaddle won't work on me. If I were so 'good' then I would not want a stranger in my granddaughter's bedroom."

"Jakob and I have a plan to help get him home..."

"Jakob!" Grandmother echoed. "Is he in on this too? How on earth did you convince *him* to bend the rules?"

"Danny is not contagious, so he's not a threat. There was no rule that said we had to report him."

"Clever little Muffin. Logic wins every time. Now that there is a direct order from Councillor Lena to find your friend and hand him over to the authorities, can you give a good explanation of why I should not do it?"

"Is Councillor Lena the tiny woman looking through that window?" Danny pointed to the screen. "She was talking about me. The Storyteller told us about the little people who lived in boxes, but none of us believed him."

We both ignored him. "Please, Grandmother, don't report him," I begged. "He got lost and had to land because he ran out of fuel. He's done nothing wrong."

"He has nothing to fear from the authorities then," she said, in a dull voice.

"Is that what your parents told you when you were four?" I choked on the words. "I don't want him taken away...like you were."

Grandmother looked at me with a wounded expression on her face. Then she turned to Danny. "Tell me about life on the mainland."

Danny scratched his head. "Where do I start? It's different from here, Ma'am, that's for sure."

"Danny hasn't even heard of cold fusion," I interrupted. "They don't know how to desalinate water, so they die when there is a drought."

Grandmother paled. "Is this true?"

"She's right," Danny agreed. "Electricity is scarce and we don't have exothermy things or running water in the houses, and no hot water comes from a tap, that's for sure. We have to scout for the things you take for granted, like windows." He tapped the silica with his fingers. "Our town is littered with useless machines that no one knows how to work."

"I didn't realise." Grandmother clutched her hand to her chest. "Otherwise, I would have done more."

"How could *you* have done more?" I asked, but Grandmother continued quizzing Danny.

"So why did you come here? Tell the truth, now."

"I wanted to help my people." Danny bowed his head. "It all started with this one thing the Storyteller told me. He gives each one of us a story when we turn thirteen. Mine was about computers. He said that when those still worked, people could go *'online'* and order things. Within a couple of days, the supplies would arrive in a truck. Except we couldn't get the computers to work, because there are no computer engineers left." He looked nervous now, his face red and sweaty. "So, I thought I would scout for one – an engineer, that is."

I burst out laughing. "You think all it takes is to turn on a computer and you can have things delivered? Who is going to make the things in the first place? Where does the delivery man come from, or were you expecting tiny delivery men the size of Councillor Lena?" I laughed harder at that thought, then I saw his face and stopped.

"You think this is funny? I don't know how computers work! I just wanted to help. I took the Scouter and the map when my dad wasn't looking. If I go back empty-handed, I'll get the flogging of my life!"

"You'd get beaten?" The thought of it jolted through my body.

"You bet!"

"May I see your map?" Grandmother interrupted.

Danny grabbed his bag from under the bed, opened it, and brought out the scarf. Tangled up in it were the metal bracelets joined by a chain. The last time I had seen them, they'd been on the front seat of the plane. He must have taken them before we left the meadow. But why would he bring them with him?

Grandmother stared at the object. "Handcuffs..." she whispered.

"How do you know what they are called? And what are they for anyway?" I asked.

"They are for restraining someone, like a rope, so the person cannot get away."

I shuddered as I imagined the metal tight around my hands and being taken somewhere I didn't want to go. I lifted my eyes to Danny's face. Both his ears were bright red. Then I understood.

"You said you wanted an engineer! That's why you wanted to be alone with Jakob all the time!" It took all my restraint not to shout. "You were planning to take him! Even after we left the meadow."

Danny kept his head down, and his face scrunched up. "I figured no Engineer would come with me of his own free will," he mumbled.

"But we were helping you! All that time you were planning to tie those things on him and force him back to the mainland! How could you?"

"I didn't know you then." His eyes avoided mine.

"Maybe I should cally Jakob and let him know your plan." I slipped the calpad off my wrist and thrust the screen into his face. "Let's see how long he'll keep your secret when he knows that the whole time you were scheming to betray him."

"I'm sorry, Astie." Danny's eyes glistened with tears. "At first all I could think was how much we needed an engineer back home. When I got to know you and Jakob, and you became my friends, I realised I couldn't go through with it. I wouldn't have kidnapped Jakob. Honest."

Grandmother broke the silence in the room. "I believe you, Danny," she said. "It's not a bad thing to want the best for your family. We've all done things we regret. Right, Astie?"

I nodded reluctantly.

"And think," she said to me, "if your family was in need and you had a way of helping them, wouldn't you do it?"

"In a flash," I agreed. My hands relaxed a little.

"You can't contact Jakob, anyway." Grandmother reached out and took my calpad. "These have tracking devices inside them and ways of registering specific words. I don't think the technology is used all the time, but tonight the Monitors are sure to be listening. If you mention Danny, they will be over here before you can blink."

"I never knew that!"

"Do you mean that your sheriffs know everything you say by listening to your machine, even when it is in your hand?" asked Danny.

"Sort of," Grandmother explained. "I know a bit about it, because my father helped to design the system. All calpad exchanges are collected in a central computer and a computer operator can track whatever he likes. If children are lost, for example, they can be located though their calpads. It also means the operators can access other information, even without your consent, and track you wherever you go."

"That's horrible!" Danny exclaimed. "How can you live like that? Imagine if the sheriffs back home knew everything I did!"

"Maybe when you leave," I said, only half-joking, "I could throw away my calpad and come with you."

Suddenly, a piercing alarm filled the air. I jumped. Had someone heard me say that? Then it dawned on me. It was the automatic front door registering an unauthorised entry.

20

Captured!

Blue Tail leapt from the bed and shot out the window, with Danny right behind her, trying to follow the cat's example. My door slid open and people in yellow biohaz suits swarmed the room. Their hoods and respirator masks that only revealed their eyes made them look like creatures out of Space Seekers.

"Please stay calm!" a woman's voice ordered, sounding raspy through her respirator. "Code Red One protocol is being instigated. For your safety, come with us."

"No way!" Danny yelled at a Monitor who had grabbed his legs and was pulling him back into the room.

Grandmother held up her calpad with Danny's stats. "This is not necessary…" she tried to explain, but a Monitor took the calpad and dropped it into a container that sealed itself on impact.

"Stop it! He's not contagious!" I said, but the Monitor pushed me aside and I fell onto the bed.

I sat stunned and watched as Danny thrashed and wriggled and screamed words I had never heard before. His cap came off and his tangled long hair made him look like a wild thing. Then he spun his head and bit hard into the man's arm. I knew it could not have hurt too much with the suits being so thick, but even so, the man let go in shock. Sure, young children bit each other before they learnt proper manners, but for a person over five to bite another was unthinkable. Danny followed up with a kick in the groin and squirmed free, but before he could escape out the window, he slumped to the floor unconscious.

"Danny!" I howled, even though I knew what had happened. The Monitor had used a nerve pinch at his neck: a grip taught to martial arts masters. I had heard about it, but never seen it done before. The Monitor picked up Danny's limp body, rolled him over his shoulder and stomped out of the room.

"I want to go with him!" I yelled, but the woman who spoke to us before stood in my way. "You are coming with us," she said, in the same firm voice.

"Surely that is not necessary!" Grandmother pulled me to her.

"Code *2.3.1 You must go into isolation immediately*!" the woman recited from the rulebook. "Surrender your calpad, please."

I looked at Grandmother and she nodded, so I snapped it off my wrist and handed it over.

Four Monitors came up close behind us and marched us down the hall.

As we left the house, I heard Mother shout, "Astatine!" I saw a Monitor pushing her into the back of a van. I could make out the shape of Father and Jon, already seated in there.

"No, no!" I wanted to scream, but all I managed was a whisper. "They didn't do anything. They didn't even know!" A Monitor slammed the back door of the van and my family was out of sight.

People in biohaz suits were erecting a large bright yellow plastic dome over our house. I couldn't believe how fast this was happening! How did they know Danny was at my place?

I looked down the street towards Jakob's house. A couple of our neighbours stood huddled in clusters, watching a yellow plastic tent being raised over Jakob's house as well.

He must have reported Danny after all. It was the logical thing to do.

Just like that, all the fight left my body. Like a droid without emotions, I let myself be hoisted into the back of the van and sat like a statue as Grandmother climbed in beside me. The door closed and she settled next to me, stroking my hair.

"It will be okay, Muffin," she murmured, but I didn't believe her. Sometimes lies are not worth the effort. Through the barred window of the van, I watched Monitors trample the lawn. Past them, through a gap in the yellow plastic I could see the front door of my house, and then even that closed over.

With a smooth glide, the vehicle moved and we headed for the unknown.

The silence in the back of a cold fusion van was absolute. I concentrated on my breathing and the pressure of Grandmother's arm around me to stave off panic. My fingers pressed against the metal floor, the slight vibrations a reminder that I was inside a vehicle.

What would Mother and Father be thinking? How much had they been told? I gave a desperate grunt of a laugh as I realised they would not see Space Seekers tonight. Jon would have a meltdown for sure once he realised it. Had Danny woken up yet? He must be terrified. What about Jakob? Had he been taken too?

So many lives in turmoil and all of it was my fault.

The flicker of night-lights flashed eerily into our cage as we headed down the streets, until they became fewer and fewer and darkness overtook us.

Without our calpads, we had no way of tracking the time, but I think we drove for close to an hour before stopping. The door opened and a bright light filled the van. The smell of salt in the air told me we were close to the sea.

"Please come with me," a woman in a biohaz suit wheezed through her respirator. I got to my feet and Grandmother groaned a little as she untangled herself from the floor. The woman held out a supporting hand and said, "We regret your discomfort. However, haste was vital for immediate isolation. Please be assured that during your stay with us you will have all necessary comforts."

"Stay?" I repeated. "What does that mean? How long do we have to stay here?" She did not answer me.

Grandmother and I stepped out of the van into a garage flooded with light. It was an old-fashioned design with exposed wooden beams. It had windows, but yellow plastic was flapping against the silica. The two other people in biohaz suits were walking away from us, leaving us alone with the woman. It was obvious they did not expect any trouble from a grandmother and a child. For a moment, I contemplated proving them wrong and running, but where would I go?

She ushered us through a door into a white room similar to a hospital operating theatre I had seen once on a medical exposure day. I wasn't interested much then and I liked it even less now.

"Please stand in front of that machine and face me," the woman instructed Grandmother, who did as she was told.

I had never seen her look so tired. For the first time ever, I realised how old she was. There was a hum and wide arms of white metal circled her, encasing her in a tube with her head showing. Then a clear tube lowered from the ceiling, covering the rest of her.

"Are you okay?" the woman shouted, and Grandmother's lips said yes, but I could not hear her voice.

The machine rippled with lights that circled from the top in waves. The woman stood behind a screen checking the data as it flowed in. It was all over in seconds. The humming stopped, the machine slid open and Grandmother stepped out.

"Your turn."

Without a word, I took Grandmother's place. It didn't hurt a bit.

Then she removed her helmet and respirator, revealing her tight black curls, and peeled off the yellow suit like shedding a banana skin. The label on her blue overalls underneath read, *"Senior Advisor, Infection Prevention, R.P. Okoro."*

She smiled at us. "You have not been contaminated."

"I could have told you that," I grumbled. "None of us are."

"Correct," R.P. Okoro agreed, "all have tested clear."

"So, can we go home now?"

"Negative. You are still in violation of Code Red One 1.1.1 through to 2.3.1. Follow me. I will take you to your quarters, for now. Councillor Lena will see you tomorrow morning at 01:00. "

"Gosh," Grandmother groaned. "We are getting special treatment. I haven't seen Lena in years."

"You know her?" I asked.

"Went to Learning Sessions with her until I was twelve. She didn't like me much."

"Why is that?"

We were following R.P. Okoro down a white hallway, walking past one closed door after another. I was surprised to see doorknobs on each one. Very unhygienic for a hospital.

"Lena's thesis was on security and she requisitioned my grandfather's calpad for her studies. He had died two years earlier, you see, and all his belongings came to me. I was already using the calpad and I refused her request. She's been a bit cross with me ever since."

"Huh? Why would she want your grandfather's calpad?"

"He was Elemental Island's first elected councillor. In fact, he named this place."

"Really?" I said, startled. "Why wasn't I ever told?"

"A job's a job," Grandmother shrugged. "Being a councillor is no more important to the community than Neil mowing the grass. Besides, it was all such a long time ago."

R.P. Okoro opened the last door at the end of the corridor and gestured for us to enter. The room was windowless. There was just enough space for two beds propped up against opposite walls, with a nightstand between them with a solitary white table lamp on it. On the wall to my left there was an open door. I could see a bathroom behind it.

"Good night," R.P. Okoro said, as she closed the door behind her with an odd click.

Grandmother sat down on one of the beds.

"Do you know where we are?" I asked.

She nodded. "I came here years ago with my father when I was a child. This complex is the old research facility. They were closing it down way back then. We were transitioning to cold fusion, and it was easier to build new facilities than to try to rewire this place with new technology."

I went to the door, expecting it to glide open. When it did not, I fumbled at the spherical door handle. When that didn't work, I yanked it with all my might.

"I want to get out of here!"

Grandmother sighed. "We're not going anywhere, Muffin. That door is locked."

21

Danny and the Tiny Woman in the Window

After a morning meal in our room, which we barely touched, two Monitors came for Grandmother and me. My stomach felt like a butterfly farm had moved in overnight, so I read their nametags to distract myself. Monitor Adam was young, tall and thin and had the beginnings of a moustache on his top lip. Monitor Chi was a girl with a kind face, her black hair pulled back in a tight ponytail.

They led us to a room with a sign that read "Lecture Hall." The first thing I noticed was the four large calpads covering the walls. My family sat in the front row alongside Jakob and his parents. I ran to Mother and she held me tight.

"I'm so sorry," I whispered.

I turned to Father sitting beside her and put my arms around him. He leaned over for a stiff hug and gave me a kiss on the forehead. Grandmother and I sat down. I refused to talk to Jakob. Jon glared at me, so I gave him an apologetic shrug.

"Zero Six strikes again," he snapped at me.

"I never meant for any of this to happen," I said. "I knew Danny was not contagious or I would never have brought him home…"

Mother turned to Grandmother. "Why didn't you inform us right away when you discovered the boy!?"

The door opened and Councillor Lena entered with her aide with the big moustache. I recognised him from the calcast that announced the discovery of Danny's plane. We all fell silent. Lena considered each of us in turn, her gaze resting on Grandmother a little longer. Her eyes narrowed. "Hello Hannah," she said. Grandmother nodded her head. Lena took something from her pocket. "I believe this is yours." She held up Grandmother's calpad and hesitating only for a second, she handed it to her. Then she dropped mine on the table in front of me.

"The good news is that none of you are contagious, including the off-lander."

"Where is Danny?" I startled myself by speaking.

"Shush, Astatine," Mother said, but Lena didn't seem to mind. "The off-lander will be here shortly."

She turned back to my parents. "Stephen and Daisy Sue Harvester…" Mother grimaced at her full name. "…after examining the facts, you and your son are released from blame. Along with the two of you," she said to Jakob's parents. "You will be free to leave tomorrow, however, as your homes are being fumigated as a precaution, you will spend the night on these premises."

"Why fumigate anything? I have sensitive equipment in my house," Uncle Luke argued.

"And what about my cats?" Father groaned.

"Don't worry, everything is safeguarded, but rules must be followed."

Lena sat down behind a desk out the front and motioned to Adam. "Please escort them to their rooms and bring in the off-lander."

They headed for the door as told, except Mother who remained seated. "I want to stay with Astatine."

"She will not be harmed and your mother is with her." Councillor Lena's voice was calm but firm.

"What will happen to them?" Mother reached for my hand under the table and held it.

"They will be helping us with our investigations," Lena answered. "Our citizens have the right to be fully informed of what has transpired and about the off-lander. The calpads on the walls will transmit the investigation. Watch yours for the calcast."

Mother hesitated. "Does it have to be so public?"

"Community Guideline 3.6.1 states that '*In order to safeguard the integrity of governance, transparency in all matters is essential. It is a core value that must be adopted and demonstrated at all times by every member of the Council,'*" she quoted.

Mother sagged. There was nothing more she could so for me and we both knew it.

"I'll be okay, Mother," I assured her as brightly as I could. She rose to her feet and followed the others out the door.

Danny entered a little while later, flanked by Adam. His gait was stiff. I caught a glint of plastic film and realised that he was wearing an elemental tight-suit. The suit was flexible with slow movements but became rigid if jerked or forced. I bet they put his movement setting to absolute minimum.

"Thank you, Adam," Lena said. "Please seat him with the others."

Danny did not move. He gawked at her and said, "You're not tiny at all."

Lena turned to her aide. "I thought the doctors said he was lucid."

For a second, I forgot myself and nearly giggled. Of course, Danny had only ever seen her on the screen. To him, she was the "*tiny woman in the window.*"

Danny shook his head as if to clear it and shuffled to his seat, scowling at Jakob as he passed him. Then I noticed his hair. They had cut it short! I was about to complain for his sake, but then I realised that he looked more like one of us this way. Not a stranger at all. As Grandmother said, on the elemental level we were all the same. I hoped Lena remembered that.

She nodded to her aide. "Tell the Council Members to holo-transfer to the meeting." He tapped his calpad and holograms of the elected leaders of Elemental Island appeared behind Lena, some sitting in their chairs, others standing at attention. "Turn the wall calpads to transmission mode," Lena said to Chi, before taking a deep breath.

"Citizens, neighbours and friends," she began. "I have an update for you this morning. You will be reassured to know that the driver of the flight machine has been located. As we do not believe that he had a passenger with him, the search parties for this morning have been cancelled."

I imagined people in town, having their breakfast as always, watching the calcast. Would they all be happy to have their routine restored? Were there others out there, like me, who felt disappointed to have missed out on a bit of change, a sniff of adventure?

"The driver was found last night in one of the houses in town, after the Monitors received a tip from a helpful citizen." She turned to Jakob. "I thank you," she said, "for acting in the interest of your community."

I knew the calcast would be focusing on Jakob now. Instead of sitting up and being proud, he hung his head low. So it had been him. I guess I couldn't blame him. Lying didn't come easy, unless you were like me.

"The off-lander was found in the company of Hannah Jones" – Lena frowned at Grandmother – "and her granddaughter, Astatine Harvester. Senior members of our Infection Prevention team have examined them, and have deemed them non-contagious. The off-lander seems to have suffered no ill effects from his flight. At the moment, we have no explanation for this."

Lena's aide stepped up to her, holding Danny's pack in his hand. He removed the contents and laid them out on the table in front of her, one by one: Danny's jacket with the outlandish logos, the scarf with the map on it, sunglasses, his flask, the handcuffs and a bundle of clothes.

Lena indicated the items and said, "These are the artefacts found in the possession of the driver. This" – she pointed at Danny – "is the driver himself."

She addressed him. "What is your name, off-lander?"

"I'm Danny Scouter, Ma'am."

"You may call me Lena. Where do you come from, Danny Scouter?" Her voice was stern.

"A town called Orange Grove. On the mainland."

"And you flew here, in this machine?" She tapped the calpad on her wrist and a 3D image of the Tiger Moth appeared.

Danny nodded. "Yes, Ma'am...I mean Lena. That's the Scouter."

"And your second name is also Scouter?"

"We are named after what we do," Danny explained. If I baked bread, I would be Danny Baker."

Lena nodded. "That is logical."

"Sometimes we are named after what we look like. You would be Lena Little, and you" – he turned to Monitor Adam – "would be Adam Zapple."

Adam frowned. "Do you call Monitors 'Zapples' where you come from?" he asked.

It took a moment for me to understand, then I saw Adam swallow and his Adam's apple bobbed like a ball under his skin. I chuckled but stopped when Grandmother nudged me.

Lena pressed on. "Are you named after your flying vehicle then?"

"Not really. The plane is named after what we do too. We scout for things."

"Is that why you came here?"

Danny shook his head. "I got lost. I ran out of fuel and had to land."

Lena unfolded the scarf in front of her.

"This scarf belongs to you, am I right?" Danny swallowed and then he nodded. Lena indicated a patch cross-stitched in black yarn on the scarf. "Is this our island here?"

Danny considered the incriminating black blob. "Um, yes."

"And do you know how to read maps? Can you use this to help you find your way home?"

Danny nodded reluctantly.

"So, you were not entirely lost then?" She pressed her calpad again to show a 3D image of two grey metal canisters lined up in the grass. "Do you recognise these?" Before Danny could answer, she added, "They were found in your 'Scouter.' They contain gasoline, which is the fuel your engine uses, according to the engineers who have examined it."

Danny shifted in his chair and scratched the side of his neck.

"You weren't telling us the truth about being lost, or being out of fuel, were you?"

"No, Ma'am," Danny whispered.

I looked at Jakob. The stunned expression on his face told me he realised Danny had been lying to us as well. I imagined how angry he would be, if he knew that it had all been part of a plan to snatch him.

"I don't know what your town is like, but in our community lying carries consequences." Lena sounded a lot less calm now. I hoped she would never find out how good I was at bending the truth.

"Come on, Lena!" Grandmother's voice startled me. I had taken it for granted that we would only speak when the Councillor addressed us, but Grandmother had a different idea. "He is a child, and a frightened one at that. Naturally, he'll tell you what he thinks you want to hear."

"You haven't changed a bit, have you?" Lena lifted her hand to silence Grandmother. "Still a law unto yourself."

"Why should I be intimidated by you of all people? Because you are the Councillor? That is an honour, but it doesn't put you above me."

Lena waved her hand. "This is pointless. His age is irrelevant, since he was old enough to find Elemental Island *and* fly here on his own." She turned back to Danny. "What were you scouting for? Were you planning to steal food?" Danny bit his lip, but didn't say anything. Her features hardened. "Technology?"

Lena leaned forward. "You are not helping your case by refusing to talk to me. What are you hiding? Are you a spy? Are there more of you coming?"

A long silence followed. It scared me. If he didn't answer, what would they do to him?

22

The Butterfly Kiss

I watched Danny's pale frightened face until I could bear it no longer. "He was looking for a computer engineer," I blurted out.

"Shut up, Astie," Danny hissed. "They'll laugh at me."

"What would you want with a computer engineer?" Lena asked.

Danny pressed his lips together, so I answered for him. "He heard a story about how in the past people ordered things by using computers and then those things arrived at your doorstep. The computers are all broken where he comes from so he thought if he found a computer engineer to fix them, they could order things again."

The aide snorted and I imagined people all over the island chuckling as they bit into their toast. I tried to catch Danny's eyes to apologise for embarrassing him, but he did not look up.

Lena nodded. "This is a logical conclusion with the limited information you possessed, Danny Scouter, and it would take a lot of bravery to seek out this solution for the need of your community."

Danny seemed surprised at her reaction.

"Now, believing that an engineer could help you, you planned to come here and ask one to return with you in your flight machine. Is this correct?"

Danny glanced at Grandmother and me and mumbled, "Sort of."

Grandmother got out of her seat, went to the table with Danny's things, and held up the handcuffs.

Danny yelled, "Don't..."

"This is going to come out soon enough anyway," Grandmother said. "Danny was prepared to kidnap an engineer if necessary and restrain that person with these handcuffs."

There was a collective gasp in the room and Jakob jumped to his feet. "You were going to snatch *me*!" he shouted. "I thought you were my friend."

"Sit down, Jakob." Grandmother's voice was firm. "The very fact that you are still here shows that he did not go through with this plan. Don't judge him too harshly, before you get some idea of why this child was so desperate to get the services of an engineer."

Lena pursed her lips. "Any judgement here will be fair and balanced. Danny, can you please tell us why you contemplated such a thing?"

"All our engineers died and so there was no one to fix our computers."

"All of them? How did they die?" Jakob asked.

"The Butterfly Kiss got them."

"The butterfly kiss?" Lena echoed.

"He's got Lepidopterophobia," Jakob explained. "He thinks butterflies make you sick."

The aide snorted again, but stifled it as a cough when Councillor Lena frowned at him. "Please tell us what you mean by saying the 'butterfly kiss got' your engineers," she asked.

"It killed them!" Danny said. "They all bit the dust. Every one of them. They died years ago and nothing has worked properly ever since."

There was stunned silence in the room.

Monitor Adam mumbled to Chi, "Did they die from butterflies or from biting dust?" Chi paid no attention to him. She was staring at Danny, her eyes glistening.

Danny continued. "You have no idea what it's like to live without engineers." He waved his hands around as he talked. "All the things you take for granted, well, we've got none of them. No invisible carpets. No skywater thingies, and sometimes no water or food. Most of our vehicles don't work and we have to scout for parts to repair things but they are never fixed properly."

"I don't understand," Lena said. "How can butterflies kill people?"

"I'm afraid he is talking of the plague," Grandmother spoke up. "The first signs were a rash like a flock of tiny butterflies patterning the skin and then the nasty side effects hit. Fever, bleeding, a breakdown of all major organs and death within forty-eight hours, with a mortality rate of 60 per cent, even higher in the young and frail. The 'Butterfly Kiss' was lethal, that's why we have quarantined Elemental Island for so many years."

Monitor Chi whispered, "Those poor people." Lena shot her a look and turned her attention back to Grandmother. "How could you know this? Did the boy tell you?"

Danny raised his hands in the air. "I didn't understand half of what she said, Ma'am, so I couldn't have told her nothing. She's right enough about the kiss though. The Storyteller tells of the Kiss, the Before and the After. It was mighty nasty and I'm glad it was gone before I was born."

Lena turned to Grandmother. "Explain how you knew about this plague."

Grandmother held up her wrist showing her calpad. "It's all in here," she began. "You know my grandfather, Councillor Ben, was one of the original settlers. When he was dying, he called me to him and gave me his calpad. 'Hannah,' he said, 'There is something I know that I cannot take to my grave. My journal is in here. Read it.' When I did, I found that it documented the early days of the Elemental Island and it mentioned the plague on the mainland."

Lena's aide said, "But that doesn't make sense. If the Elemental Harvesters knew about the plague, why isn't this taught in the Learning Hub? And..."

Lena cut in, "If *you* knew about it, why have you held back this information?"

Grandmother rubbed her head as though it was aching. "For once, I agree with you, Lena." She faced the calpad on the opposite wall, and I knew her 3D image was being projected into every home.

"My friends," she said, "The story is simple. One hundred and thirty-six years ago, Ben Jones brought a group of scientists to live here and to conduct experiments in the fields of energy and elemental harvesting. Every child has heard that in history investigation. We all know that in the beginning, they were all single to make sure they would be suited for isolation and able to focus on the task. Our records also tell of the second wave of scientists seven years later, and how we became the thriving community we are today, as people formed couples and raised children. Then, there is the part you have not been told, the one that the Elemental Harvesters allowed to pass from memory."

"You mean they kept *secrets*?" Danny raised his eyebrows.

Lena interrupted. "That's impossible. Community Guideline 3.6.1 says, *"In order to safeguard the integrity of governance, transparency in all matters is essential."* Are you telling us that they broke their own rules?"

"I'm just telling you what Councillor Ben recorded. They invited the second wave of scientists from all disciplines to give them sanctuary from the plague. My own grandmother, Lisa Flint, came during that time. Then they put in place stringent rules to protect everyone from infection, including prohibiting flight machines and watercraft from leaving. Perhaps even our reluctance to gather in groups and our fear of germs came from this era."

"Are you saying," Lena asked, "that the only reason we are forbidden to leave is because of a long gone health threat?"

"Yes."

"And flight is not harmful to the human body?"

"I wouldn't know about that, but it seems so. Ask him." Grandmother gestured to Danny.

"Is this true?" Lena said to Danny. "Flight does not cause internal damage at all?"

Danny shrugged. "Not unless you fall out of the plane."

"But Grandmother," I said, "why would the first scientists make up an untrue story about this and why has the plague been kept a secret for so long?"

Grandmother sighed. "Allowing people to forget is not quite the same as keeping a secret. Perhaps over time, people presumed the human body could not survive flight, and with no way to test it, the myth prevailed. As for the plague on the mainland, perhaps the ones who fled from it were so traumatised that they thought it better not to speak of it. Why burden their children with such a horrible history?"

"Great!" Danny huffed. "So you guys are so happy and comfortable over here that you *forgot* about how tough life is where I come from?" His jaw clenched as he spoke. "You hoarded all the engineers, knowing millions of us would die and then you left us to face the music!"

Monitor Adam whispered to Chi, "Is he saying their music kills people?"

"I think so," she nodded.

"Every day," Danny went on, "we live without clean water and electricity, with no medicines to heal us when we get sick, with no 'calpads' to do...

whatever it is calpads do!" He almost spat out that last sentence. "And now *I* am the one in trouble?"

He was right. None of it made sense. "But Grandmother," I said, "*you* didn't forget. Why didn't you tell someone when you found out?"

"You still haven't answered that question, Hannah," Lena said. "I'll ask you again, please explain why you have withheld this information from us."

"Grandfather...I mean *Councillor Ben* forbade me to say anything. By the time he was dying, the plague and the mainland was pretty much forgotten. He said we had to safeguard what the Elemental Harvesters have built up here. His life's work. He told me one day people would come from the mainland, and that would be the time to reveal what I knew. If it didn't happen in my lifetime, I should pass that knowledge on to my grandchild."

Grandmother's voice trembled. "It has been a very hard secret to keep and I am happy I won't have to pass on this burden."

She looked straight at the calpad on the wall and people all over the island would not meet her eyes. "Councillor Ben was trying to protect you all. Think about your lives, your schedules. Think how much time you are allowed to spend on the things you love because you are surrounded by every comfort that science can provide. How much of that would you be prepared to give up?"

I watched Lena and saw her swallow. Monitor Adam licked his lips.

Grandmother's voice grew stronger. "Would you put aside your thesis or special interest for a few months, *maybe years*, to travel to a place you have never been before, to meet with people you don't know, who have customs you are not familiar with? Could you live without pure water to drink whenever you liked, or regular meals or a house that is climate controlled to your exact specifications?"

She raised her voice, sounding determined. "I challenge you. Could you do these things?" She paused and I knew that in every house her question resonated.

"Perhaps it was wrong of me not to tell anyone about the plague and my fears for the mainland. In my own way, I did try to get you to travel and see for yourself what was out there."

"When did you do that?" Lena shook her head. "You have never said anything to me."

"She created Space Seekers!" I cried. "You wanted people to build flight machines and to explore places they have never been before, didn't you, Grandmother!"

She nodded. "But then, instead of becoming adventurous, they discovered Feralblasters and Snogarts."

"*Ferroblasters* and *Zogarts*," Lena, Jakob and the Monitors all corrected her at the same time.

Danny clapped his hands together slowly and everyone in the room turned to him. "Wonderful," he said with a toothy grin on his face. It was as if his lips made a happy smile but they didn't mean it. "You must be so proud that *once, long ago* you tried to tell your people that we might need help."

I knew that he meant the exact opposite of what he was saying. Grandmother knew it too and she blushed bright red. I had never seen her so uncomfortable.

Copying Grandmother, Danny turned to face the wall calpad. "Now that you know how much we need you, will you come and help my people?"

Before he could finish, the door swung open and Uncle Luke barged into the room with a Monitor behind him. "I MUST see it!" he yelled.

23

If Someone Betrays You, You Punch Them on the Nose

Lena bristled. "Please leave this room immediately!"

Uncle Luke paid her no attention and pointed at the rocket on Danny's jacket that lay on the table. "This space craft. Is it real? Does it exist?"

Danny ogled the wild man in front of him. I didn't blame him. Uncle Luke's white hair was sticking out at all angles as if he had slept on it for a week without brushing it. "Um, yes," Danny replied. "There's one not far from where I live. Some of the parts have been scavenged, but most of that thing is still there."

"And this." Uncle Luke touched the patch with the word "NASA." "Have you seen these letters anywhere?"

"Sure, I've seen that pattern before. It's all over the place."

Uncle Luke's face lit up. "I want to go to the mainland!"

Lena was lost for words as Uncle Luke continued. "My grandfather used to tell me stories that his father told him about NASA rocket ships that flew into space. I thought he was making up his own episodes of Space Seekers, but I still have a birthday card he made me one year. This exact spaceship was on the front – with NASA written in capitals!" He clutched the jacket to his chest. "I knew flight was forbidden, so I did my thesis on hover boots, but in my heart I dream of rockets."

"You can't dream in your heart," Lena corrected him, but Uncle Luke kept talking. "If I can find this ship and work out how it was built, we might be able to go into space again!"

We digested this thought in silence. Then Chi put up her hand. "I would like to go too. To help them, the people of the mainland."

Grandmother added, "I know I'm old and not much use, but if I go, perhaps I can make up for all the years I stayed silent."

Lena closed her eyes. We all awaited her verdict, except for Jakob. He stood. His face was ashen.

"Community Guideline 3.6.1 insists I be transparent in all things," he said. "For this reason

I feel it is essential that I share with you some information."

Danny and I exchanged glances. The butterflies in my stomach were swarming.

"Based on observations and information gleaned from many conversations with Danny Scouter, I believe that both he and the majority of his community suffer from extreme cases of Social Syndrome."

I sank into my chair, nauseous, my stomach churning. Jakob, how could you?

Lena bowed her head towards Jakob. "I commend you for your honesty." She turned to Danny. "Is this true?"

"I don't know what he's saying. We're social enough folks if that's what you mean."

"Do you enjoy congregating, that is, gathering together in large groups? Do you talk about illogical things? Do you often break rules?"

"Seems to me you're asking all the wrong questions, Ma'am. You forgot, 'Do you need our help?'"

Lena stiffened. "It is not your place to question my ways. You forget who I am."

She paused, and closed her eyes for a few seconds. When she opened them, she addressed the wall calpad. "I have taken all facts into consideration and possess in-depth knowledge of the relevant laws. As your head councillor, I have made my decision. Danny Scouter, please stand."

Danny got up, his movements awkward in his suit.

"You are charged with the following breaches of law. Count one, landing on Elemental Island without permission. Count two, driving a forbidden flight machine. Count three, not submitting yourself to authorities. Count four, reckless endangerment of our community by exposing us to the threat of plague. Count five, attempted abduction. I find you guilty on all counts. You will be taken into isolation for re-education."

There was a collective gasp in the room.

"No way!" Danny cried. "I didn't even know half those rules existed!"

Lena raised her hand for silence. "Ignorance of the law is no defence. Given that the mainland is a dangerous, chaotic place without basic amenities or medical facilities, populated with a people riddled with Social Syndrome most likely prone to violence and manipulation, I rule that flight should remain forbidden. No one is to leave Elemental Island."

Lena ignored the mumbling of the other councillors. "Danny Scouter, upon your release you are to become a functioning member of our society. To prevent you from revealing the community, you will never be permitted to return to the mainland. Your re-education shall begin effective immediately."

Pandemonium broke out.

"This is outrageous!" Grandmother snapped. "He's a child!"

"I want to fly!" Uncle Luke shouted.

"They don't have food and water!" Chi moaned.

At that moment, ghostly men and women popped up all over the room. People were using their calpad hologram options to "attend" the meeting.

"This might be law, but it is not justice!" an old man growled. "It's a snap decision, made without consultation or deliberation."

"We now have evidence that flight does not cause death!" a woman squawked.

"In accordance with clause 15.3.1, I hereby request that we put these decisions to a general vote," a young man said, with his rulebook in hand.

Soon there were hundreds of voices babbling at once. I put my hands over my ears to shield them from the noise. Never had people disagreed so openly about a ruling given by a councillor. Rules were obvious and went unquestioned.

"SILENCE!" Lena roared.

The holograms disappeared and Lena swallowed hard, her face pale. "It seems that there is a dissent to the ruling. As we were reminded, according to clause 15.3.1, once a decision is questioned, it may be put to a general vote, as long as someone seconds the notion."

"Seconded." It was Lena's aide. She glared at him and he shrugged. "My daughter has always dreamed of going into space." Uncle Luke gave the man a grateful grin.

"So be it," Lena affirmed. "The fact that Danny Scouter is guilty of breaking our laws is not in doubt. Therefore, there are two questions remaining. Is Danny Scouter free to leave and should flight be permissible?"

"There is a third question," Chi added. "Should we send help to the mainland?"

"Agreed," Lena nodded, facing the calpad on the wall. "Everyone will now receive these motions."

My calpad vibrated. The three questions appeared with a tick box for yes or no or undecided.

"We need a 60 per cent agreement to alter the decisions. We shall adjourn for thirty minutes while you consider the facts and record your vote."

"What? Half an hour?" Danny asked. "Skrate! You guys are fast."

"Efficiency is desirable in all things." Lena rose to her feet. "Take the children to the beach for some air while we are adjourned," she said to Adam, before walking out of the room, with her aide in tow.

We sat on the sand. Behind us, at a little distance, the two Monitors were keeping an eye on Danny. I threw shells into the foam as the surf rolled close to our feet and Danny sat immobile in his elemental suit which glimmered in the sunlight. Jakob huddled alone under a palm. A high wire fence surrounded us on three sides with the ocean open in front of us. We were caged but even if we were to run, there was nowhere to hide.

"I wish we would get a vote," I said as I picked up the remnants of a shell and hurled it at the waves. "It's not fair that adults alone get to decide on things."

"Grown-ups are the bosses back home too. At least we have that in common," Danny said.

"I'd be in there voting, if this was happening next week."

"How come?"

"I turn twelve in three days. If I select a thesis by then, I will be considered an adult. Rule 221."

"That's kind of like our initiation. Except we do it at thirteen. Maybe those of us with *social syndrome,* whatever that is, and you guys are not that different after all."

"I am sort of social," I whispered.

"I guessed that long ago. You are the only one I've met here that I feel comfortable around." He reached out, gave my hand a squeeze and did not let go. I surprised myself by leaning my head on his shoulder. If this was a symptom of SoS then I wouldn't give it up for anything.

"I apologise for the distress I caused you…" said a voice behind us.

I sprang away from Danny as Jakob loomed over us.

"…however, rules must be obeyed," he said as he sat down next to me, leaving a healthy personal space.

"We've got rules where I come from too, brah," Danny said. "If someone betrays you, you punch them on the nose."

"And yet, my nose is unharmed. That means I am better at keeping rules than you are," Jakob noted.

"I can soon fix that!" Danny said and tried to jump to his feet, but the elemental suit slowed him down and he fell onto the sand. The suit glistened as he struggled upright and reached out to grab Jakob in slow motion, like a Space Seekers alien.

He broke into a grin. "If you stay still for half an hour, then your nose will be well and truly punched!" He sank back onto the dune.

"Would it have been better if our people flew to your land, unaware of the Social Syndrome epidemic there?" Jakob asked as he ran some silky hot sand through his hands.

"We haven't got an epidemic. The plague has been gone for years!"

"Perhaps there was a gene mutation that was passed through generations, or there is a lingering effect that makes you all suffer from the same disease," Jakob suggested. "Whatever the cause, I surmise that if you are typical of your people, then anyone who goes to the mainland will be lied to, manipulated and threatened with violence on occasion. Is that correct?"

Danny opened his mouth to object, and then clenched his fists in his lap. "Maybe, a bit, but we're not *that* bad. Besides, we need your help."

"Undoubtedly," he agreed. 'But do *we* need *you*?"

A gust of wind swept spray over our faces. I imagined Danny's world, where fresh water could not come from the sea, where people died from things we could fix in a flash, and I said softly, "Sometimes, the best logic is to do the right thing because it is the right thing to do." I put my hand next to his on the ground. "Jakob, I have Social Syndrome."

His breathing quickened. I didn't dare look at him, so I counted the waves hitting the shore. When I reached forty-two, I felt his little finger touch mine.

"Astie, remember when I told you, you had one friend, and that without me your life would be 100 per cent worse?" I nodded.

He stared at the ocean. "Without you, my life would be 100 per cent worse too."

Adam called out, "Time is up." I half-expected Jakob to yank his hand away at the Monitor's voice, but instead he reached out and squeezed my fingers, before he got up.

We filed back into the conference hall and sat down. Lena was the last to arrive. We watched on the wall calpad as the computer tallied up the votes. The numbers were final. They were on the screen for all to see.

I forgot to breathe. Grandmother choked back a sob.

"What?" Danny said, his voice shaking.

Of course! He couldn't read the results. Before I could say anything, Uncle Luke gave a hoot of joy. Danny looked at me and I nodded. A huge smile spread across his face, showing off the gap in his teeth. My heart felt like it would explode. Danny was safe. Flight was permissible. We were free to leave Elemental Island.

Mainland here I come!

24

The Adventurers of Elemental Island

For three days after the ruling, Grandmother and I worked on my thesis application. I slept at her house so we could continue late into the night. Her living room was strewn with velvet, lace and leather. I don't think we could have done it without Jakob. He was being extra nice to me. At first, I was annoyed, thinking he treated me as if I was sick or something, now that he knew I had SoS. I played on that big time and told him if he wanted to help me, then he could make sure the 3D printer kept running while Grandmother and I slept. When I got up in the morning and he proudly presented my newest designs, I knew I had my friend back. More than that, I had never lost him.

On the day of my twelfth birthday, wearing a long lab coat, I stood in front of Teacher and the

Learning Hub Council. Grandmother and Mother watched from behind a curtain. Father stayed home because he didn't want to leave his cats, as they were still unsettled from the Monitors rushing through our house. He also had to keep an eye on Blue Tail, who hadn't yet assimilated into the clowder. Jon's schedule was already full so he didn't come either. Danny was busy with flight scientists who had a million questions to ask him. Okay, I admit – a slight exaggeration there. Jakob stood off stage, his face extra still, so I knew he was nervous. I had said to him that he had to make up for telling on Danny by being my assistant at the presentation. I refused to listen to why that was not logical.

"Honourable guests," I began, "I would like to present my application for a Thesis in Wearable Science."

After a gentle nudge from Grandmother, Jakob walked on stage wearing an exact replica of Danny's bomber jacket, complete with NASA logo and rocket ship emblem. He stood with his arms stiff beside him. I could have used holograms, but this was much more fun.

"This jacket," I announced, "is made from elemental fabric. It is light, strong, and has its own built-in thermostat, Medihealth function, not to forget the option to change its colour should you want to co-ordinate with your shoes and bags."

Jakob touched the lapel to demonstrate and the jacket turned yellow, black and blue in quick succession.

Teacher nodded in appreciation, but I was only getting started. With Grandmother, Mother and Jakob as my models, I revealed decorated T-shirts that read the nutrients of the food the wearer was digesting, trousers that measured the energy consumed and the distance a person walked, and a dress that changed colour to indicate lowered resistance and a heightened risk for contracting a virus. Finally, I slipped off my lab coat and was rewarded by the shocked faces of the Council.

I was wearing Grandmother's original spacesuit designed for Space Seekers, complete with bead-encrusted sleeves and stone buttons.

"This suit can measure oxygen levels, atmospheric pressure, temperature and body functions," I explained as I tapped hidden panels to reveal displays. "And as such, it is perfect for travel in an open-air flight machine."

One of the men on the council clapped quietly. Soon the others joined in and the room vibrated with praise. I had to wait a short time while the council members murmured between them, then Teacher came up beside me.

"Astatine Harvester, the decision is unanimous. Your thesis is approved. I now pronounce you a full member of the community. Well done."

Grandmother rushed on stage to envelop me in her arms.

"Are you going to apply to become one of The Adventurers?" a council member called out.

It had been a given that the first wave of flight machines to the mainland would be called The Adventurers, after the first episode of Space Seekers.

I held up my wrist and tapped enter. The application form I had already completed appeared on the room's calpad screen.

"I've been ready to send this for a very, very long time," I said as I pressed "submit."

"The application has only been available since yesterday," Teacher pointed out.

I just smiled.

The permit came two days later, in an ordinary cally. I read the sentences over and over again, realising for the first time just how much my life was about to change.

"That old machine is not proven to be safe," Mother said with a frown when I told her that I intended to fly in the Tiger Moth with Danny.

"Don't worry, Mother," Jon said. "If flight causes brain damage then it will improve her. Perhaps I will have to call her Zero Seven when she comes back."

"Don't insult your sister," Mother said automatically, but it hit me how much I would miss his teasing.

"Astatine can decide for herself. She's a clever girl." Father surprised us all. He rarely expressed an opinion on anything that wasn't cat-related.

And so, I decided for myself.

On the day of departure, I stood on the beach road, dressed in my flight suit. The Tiger Moth had been towed there, since it needed a long flat strip of land to be able to take off, and we didn't have many of those on the island. Hundreds of people came out to watch and if I hadn't been so excited, tense, scared and exhilarated, I would have marvelled at such a large group together at one time.

Although many had come to see us off, there was just one other flight machine there, the disc-shaped hope machine from Beach Park that Jakob and I played on as children. It could take four people, and Grandmother and Monitor Chi were to fly with Uncle Luke and an engineer whose thesis was on ancient machinery. Blue Tail was on board there too. Danny had muttered something about how they could use another ratter back home, but no matter how much he tried to hide it, I knew he had grown fond of that stray.

"Where are all the others?" I asked Jakob as I scanned the skies waiting for more to arrive. Councillor Lena had decreed that all inventors of flight vehicles could have a cold fusion engine allocated for their hope machines and those wishing to accompany Danny were to meet here at 02:00 today. "I thought more people would want to help those on the mainland? At the very least, those with flight obsessions would be keen to test their machines, wouldn't they?"

"They can test their machines without leaving," Jakob countered. "Without having to interact with strangers."

"You mean with people who have SoS, because we are so scary and dangerous," I snapped at him.

"Astatine," he said so gently that I forgave him for using my full name, "if having SoS makes you the person you are, then I wish we all had a bit of it."

My jaw dropped. Literally. No idiom required. Jakob didn't see though as he stared at the ground. Because he wasn't expecting it, my hug almost toppled him. "Jakob," I said, "You are the best cousin I have ever had."

"I am your *only* cousin. I will miss you and all your crazy ways. Remember your obsession with fairy tales that drove everyone mad for months? Well, I am glad that you found a prince to save you from the tower in the end."

"Huh! He's hardly a prince. Besides, I am the one saving Danny!"

"That's right! Don't ever let him forget it." Jakob flashed a half-smile. "Keep safe, Astie."

Danny marched up and grabbed Jakob's hand and shook it, pumping it up and down. Poor Jakob. He would need extra time in the Sensory Park to de-stress after today.

"Goodbye, brah. And good luck with your thesis."

"Perhaps you will get to see it," Jakob said, retracting his hand. "I am considering applying for the mainland once I turn twelve in forty-six days."

"Really?" I leapt forward to hug Jakob again, but he stepped back just in time.

"That's great, brah. We need people like you." Danny patted Jakob softly on the back.

"I understand you require more engineers."

"Nah, well, yes, we do. But I mean you are honest and upfront. I know where I stand with you. Which is more than I can say for most people I know. And you could teach me some of your self-defence moves."

Jakob nodded. "Perhaps that could be arranged." He gave an awkward smile and a quick wave and walked away.

"Do you have everything, Astatine?" Father was right behind me, wearing one of my T-shirts which had a Space Seeker rocket ship on it with the words *"I need my space"*.

Mother and Jon stood on either side of him. I nodded and tried to get rid of the lump in my throat.

"It's almost time, Astie. Do you think anyone else will come?" Danny said.

"Probably not," Jon replied for me. "I can't imagine why people would want to go to a land where everyone is like Astatine." Then he winked at me, and I knew he loved me deep down.

"Well, then, one plane is better than none and I *am* bringing back an engineer, so I should escape that flogging from dad. We need to make a move. We have to get there before dark." Danny went back to his machine and started the pre-flight checks.

I turned to Mother and she wrapped her arms around me with tears in her eyes. "Astatine, you are precious and unique. Come home safe, my daughter."

Father squeezed me so tight I knew he'd been skipping his contact etiquette classes.

"Astie! Come on!" Danny called. He was already sitting in the back seat of the Tiger Moth. He wore a bizarre leather cap that tied under his chin and a huge pair of goggles. Nothing could convince him that the elemental helmet I was wearing was lighter and better. "I'm not putting on no plastic suit ever again," had been his exact words.

I climbed up on the wing and stood a moment to survey the crowd. My home. The land I was leaving. Was I ready? I gave a huge wave. I was born ready for this.

I slid into the narrow confines of the passenger seat, then leaned out so I could see everyone. Councillor Lena pulled hard on the propeller and it swung around. The engine spluttered into action. She leaped back and put her hands to her ears, as did many in the crowd. My helmet muffled the noise but I heard Danny's voice clearly in my ear via the two-way transmitter Jakob had modified for us.

"Buckle up, sweetheart!"

I clicked on my seat belt and we rumbled down the road. The disc-shaped machine that contained Grandmother and Uncle Luke hovered in the air beside us and I waved, knowing they could see out even if I could not see in.

I fell back with a whoop of joy, squashed into my seat as we left the ground and wobbled into the air. We were flying! The Tiger Moth arched in the air and I leaned out as far as the belt would let me. People pointed and waved.

"Look!" Danny's voice rang in my ear and I swivelled in my seat. The sky below us was teeming with flight machines. Twirling spheres and long tubes with propellers rose from every corner of town. There was even one made of transparent elemental titanium and I gaped at the crew who seemed to be floating mid-air.

The Tiger Moth shot straight into the air and we looped the loop in the sky.

"Woohoo!" I hooted. "The world looks skrate upside down!"

Danny laughed and we headed out to sea for the long curve of the horizon.

by the same author

Blue Bottle Mystery – The Graphic Novel

An Asperger Adventure

Kathy Hoopmann

Illustrated by Rachael Smith

Adapted by Mike Medaglia

ISBN 978 1 84905 650 2

eISBN 978 1 78450 204 1

Everything is going wrong for Ben. His teacher is angry all the time, mostly at him. He is bullied and no one understands him, not even his own father. Then everything changes the day Ben and his friend, Andy, discover an old blue bottle in the school yard. What mysterious forces have they unleashed? In the midst of it all, Ben is diagnosed with Asperger Syndrome, and he, his family and Andy begin a journey of discovery, understanding and acceptance.